Tony is hiding. He might have managed to escape from the people who were torturing him, but while his body has healed, his mind hasn't. The memories haunt him, and he can't trust anyone, not even his dearest friends.

How can he trust his mate?

Sam didn't expect to find his mate in the council assassins. He's always been wary of the profession, even though both his parents and his siblings have made it a family business. He can't entirely avoid them, though, just like he can't avoid his mate when he meets him.

Tony has no idea how to deal with having Sam in his life when he can't even allow his mate to come close to him, but thankfully, Sam isn't easily pushed away. No matter how slow their progress is, he's not going anywhere.

Will Tony be able to heal from the trauma when the people who hurt him are still out there and a threat to him and the people he considers his family? Or will he have to do something radical to make sure he and Sam have a future together?

This book is a work of fiction. Names, characters, places, and incidents either are products of the author's imagination or are used fictitiously. Any resemblance to actual events or locales or persons, living or dead, is entirely coincidental.

Tony
Copyright © 2021 Catherine Lievens
ISBN: 978-1-4874-3178-5
Cover art by Angela Waters

Published by eXtasy Books Inc or
Devine Destinies, an imprint of eXtasy Books Inc

Look for us online at:
www.eXtasybooks.com or www.devinedestinies.com

Tony
Council Assassins 12

By

Catherine Lievens

CHAPTER ONE

Tony wanted to go back to the warehouse. That was impossible since it had been compromised, but he needed his own space. He loved Miles and his family and the fact that they'd welcomed him when he needed a place to stay, but this wasn't his home.

Tony was a burden, but he supposed he always would be from now on. He didn't think he could be a council assassin anymore, not after what had happened to him. He'd been captured and tortured, and this was the result. Tony was terrified of everything and anything, and he doubted that would change anytime soon.

A knock on what was now his bedroom door made him jump. "Tony?" Miles called out.

Tony forced himself to relax. Miles was his best friend. He wouldn't hurt him, and Tony knew that. His mind and body didn't share that opinion, though. Since he'd come back, he was even afraid of Miles. He loathed feeling like this, but no matter how many times he told himself he shouldn't, it didn't make a difference. "Yes?" he answered.

"Are you ready?"

Tony swallowed. As much as he disliked being a burden for Miles and his family, he also didn't want to leave this house. It had been a safe place for him since the warehouse had been attacked. He and the others couldn't go back to it, but they'd found a new place to turn into a home, and today, they'd started moving in.

Tony felt he shouldn't be. He'd been a council assassin for

1

years, but he couldn't be one anymore. He couldn't go on missions, not when he was afraid of his own shadow. Did he really deserve a room in the warehouse? The assassins had been his family for a long time, and they still were. That didn't change the fact that Tony couldn't continue working with them. He wasn't sure where that left him. He didn't have a life outside the assassins, and he didn't want one. He wanted to be alone as much as he wanted to be with his friends, but that wasn't possible, either.

"Tony?" Miles asked again.

Whatever decision Tony made, he couldn't ignore Miles. It wouldn't be fair, not when Miles was more like his brother than his friend, not when he'd been the one helping and supporting Tony since he'd come back.

Tony cleared his throat. "I'll be right there," he promised.

There was a pause before Miles answered. "You don't have to come today if you don't want to. We're just starting to move things, but we're not actually moving in apart from a few of us."

Tony bristled. "I said I'd be right there," he snapped. He pressed his lips together. He'd been snapping too often, pushing away the only people who cared about him. That needed to stop, but he wasn't sure *how* to make it stop. "I'm sorry. I'm coming, though."

"All right. I'll be waiting for you downstairs. Take your time."

Tony hated all of this. He wanted to go back to his old life, to a time when he wasn't afraid of his own shadow. Miles was the only one who knew how bad things had become, and Tony didn't want to be exposed that way to the others. They were his family, and they wouldn't care, but this wasn't their job.

It was more than that, though. Tony didn't want the others to see him this way and realize he couldn't be part of their family anymore, but he also didn't want to be vulnerable. Being in a new warehouse, leaving the bedroom he'd been in since he'd arrived at Miles's parents' house, meant exposing himself to danger. It meant someone could kidnap him the way they had on his last mission.

He still had nightmares about it.

But he couldn't stay where he was. This wasn't his home, and Miles's parents had already done more than enough for him. They deserved to have their home back to themselves.

Even though it cost him a lot, Tony got to his feet. He looked around, but there was nothing else he needed to do in this bedroom. He only had a few things from the warehouse he and the other assassins had lived in. He'd been wounded and in pain when he'd left, and he didn't have the energy to go back. Miles had grabbed him a few more things, but everything fit into one backpack, and Tony had already packed it. He snatched it from the end of the mattress and hauled it onto his shoulder, then turned to the closed bedroom door.

He stood in front of it, breathing deeply. He could already feel a hint of panic growing in his chest, but he couldn't give in. He needed to do this, and he needed to appear calm and in control as he did it. He sucked in a breath, then, with a trembling hand, he reached for the door handle.

Miles had said he was going downstairs, but instead, he was in the hallway, waiting for Tony. He was leaning against the wall, his arms crossed over his chest, and he smiled when he saw Tony. His smile faded a few seconds later, though, and Tony knew he hadn't done a good job hiding his feelings.

"What's going on?" Miles asked.

Tony hesitated. He didn't want to tell Miles what he'd been thinking, but Miles would push. That was just the kind of person he was. "I'm nervous," he finally admitted, even though that was far from being the entire truth.

Miles slowly nodded. "I see. What are you nervous about?"

"What *aren't* I nervous about? I'm nervous about everything, Miles."

"You'll be safe. I called Win, and the security system is already in place. We have several generators this time, so no one else will be able to sneak in or attack. It's a fortress."

"Julian isn't who I'm worried about," Tony pointed out.

"No one is, but still. It's better if we can avoid something like that happening again." Miles paused and looked straight at Tony. "And you won't be taken a second time. I'll make sure of it."

Tony snorted softly. "I was taken on a mission. You couldn't have done anything."

"Maybe not, but I still feel like I should have. I don't want to talk about that right now, but we will if it helps you."

"I doubt anything can help me. What am I doing? I can't be an assassin anymore. You saw me. I've been hiding here since we arrived, and there's no way I'll be able to go on a mission on my own again. I don't deserve a spot at the warehouse or with the council assassins."

Miles looked like he wanted to slap Tony, and knowing him, he probably did. "Don't talk like that," he said, pointing his index finger at Tony's face. "You might not have been working recently, but no one has been. All missions have been paused until we move into the warehouse."

"That's not what I was talking about. Now that we're moving, everyone else will go back to work. I can't."

"Then you'll stay home."

"It's not fair."

"It doesn't have to be. We're not just assassins. We don't only work for the council. We're also a family, and everyone wants you there, even if you never go on another mission. We don't care about that."

He was right. Tony didn't want to lose the only people he trusted. He would put his life into any of the assassins' hands, which was what he was about to do. That was one thing he wasn't afraid of. He knew everyone would keep him safe and that they would have nothing to say about the fact that his capture had left him the way he was.

There was nothing Tony could do to change. Either he went with Miles and settled in, or he left and found himself a new place to stay, new friends, a new family. He couldn't do that. He loved the assassins, and they *would* keep him safe. If he were on his own, though, he would be vulnerable, and he never wanted to feel like that again.

He only had two choices, and it wasn't hard to make his decision. "Let's go."

Sam was already regretting agreeing to help his brother move.

He wasn't sure why he had. Julian had plenty of friends who could help him, and he and Sam weren't that close. They loved each other now, even though, as children, they'd spent most of their time fighting.

Sam smiled as he remembered the time he'd written his brother's name on the wall and had tried to blame him for it. He hadn't realized Julian had been too short to reach that spot, and he'd ended up the one in trouble. Somehow, Julian always seemed to manage to get his way out of whatever he got himself into. It was something Sam admired, and something his brother needed, considering the kind of job he'd chosen.

Sam and Julian were very different, and Sam felt awkward every time he had to deal with Julian. The same went when it came with the rest of their family. Sam was the black sheep, and he often felt like he didn't entirely belong. Or maybe, in this case, he was the *white* sheep. Every member of his family had at one point worked as a professional killer, including

Sam's mother. She was retired now, although she'd been making noises about going back to work since she didn't have children to take care of anymore. The thought made Sam shudder, and he pushed it away. Yes, he *was* the family's white sheep, and he didn't want anything to do with their jobs. That didn't mean he didn't love them, though, which was one of the reasons he'd agreed to help Julian and his mate.

The other was that he was curious.

Sam had never wanted to be a professional assassin, but he was curious about Julian's new job. No one in their family had ever worked for the council. They'd known about the council assassins' existence, just like everyone in the business, but Julian was the first to work for them. He'd been quiet about it, and Sam suspected he was hiding something. That wasn't surprising, since the council assassins were supposed to be secret. That was one of the reasons he was curious to see the place where they would live. He was also touched that both Julian and the assassins trusted him enough to welcome him there.

A banging on the door made him glare at it. Julian had never been subtle, and that wasn't going to change, even though Julian's entire life had.

Sam strode to the door, throwing it open. He scowled at Julian, who was standing on the porch, grinning. "Do you know how expensive buying a house is? I don't want to have to replace the door."

Julian beamed. "I would help you. I didn't break it, though."

"I'm surprised you didn't, with how hard you were knocking."

"I wanted to make sure you heard me, what with you being older and everything."

Sam took a deep breath. *This* was one of the reasons he had as few interactions with his brother as possible. "I'm only fifty-four." Which, for a shifter, was nothing.

The smile didn't fade from Julian's lips. "That's what I said. You're old."

"You're forty-nine! That's only five years younger than me."

"And so much prettier. Are you ready?"

Sam still had time to rethink this. He could say he had a work emergency. He could tell Julian he couldn't go with him anymore, and even though Julian would be disappointed, he would accept it. Besides, he was used to Sam having work emergencies. It didn't sound like it, but it often happened in the real estate world.

But Sam had made a promise, and even though he never quite knew how to act around his brother, he wanted to spend time with him. Sam had always made sure everyone knew he was different from the rest of his family, but that was one of the reasons he sometimes felt like he wasn't part of it. It was a feeling that didn't sit well with him, but he couldn't change how he felt about what they did.

"We can go," he confirmed.

He hadn't thought it possible, but Julian's smile stretched even wider. He stepped forward and wrapped his arms around Sam, squeezing so hard Sam had trouble breathing. "I'm happy you agreed to help. I can't wait to spend time with you."

"I only agreed because you made puppy eyes."

Julian let go and looked up at Sam.

There were the puppy eyes again.

"If I'd known how weak you are against them, I would have used them a while ago."

"You've been using them since you were two. Are we ready to go, then?"

"Whenever you are. My mate is waiting." Julian gestured

toward the front yard, and Sam looked up to see a blond man standing on the grass. He was staring at them, and he smiled when he noticed Sam looking back.

Sam cleared his throat. He wasn't sure how to behave with Julian, and the same went for Julian's mate, Tali. He and Tali barely knew each other, although Sam supposed this was the opportunity to change that. Julian was in Sam's life forever, which meant that so was his mate. Sam needed to get to know Tali, and hopefully, they would at least not hate each other.

He stepped back into the house, grabbed his cell phone, wallet, and keys, then went back to the porch. Julian was still there, bouncing on the balls of his feet. It was good to see him so happy, but Sam still felt the need to warn him. "I might have to go to work."

Julian rolled his eyes. "When *don't* you have to go to work? You know, I'm not sure you chose the right job. You could have gone into the family business like I did."

Sam grimaced. "I don't want to talk about that." They already had, and plenty of times. Every time there was a family reunion, they talked about how Sam had stepped out of the family business to become a real estate agent. It had become part of Christmas and birthdays traditions, and Sam wished it hadn't.

Julian pouted. "You never want to talk about that. I just don't understand how you can think being a real estate agent is interesting."

"And I don't understand how you can think that killing people for a living is interesting or something anyone should do."

Julian shrugged. "Some people deserve to die."

"And everyone deserves a home to live in."

Julian arched a brow. "Touché."

Sam blinked. "I'm sorry?" When had Julian started speaking French?

"You're right. I still think that selling houses is boring, but if you like it, be my guest. I'm not going to stop being an assassin just because you disapprove, and I suppose the same goes for you."

Sam looked around. "Okay. Who are you, and what have you done with my brother?"

Tali laughed from the yard, and Julian turned around to glare at his mate. It made Sam smile, but he made sure the smile was gone by the time Julian turned back to face him.

"I'm no different than I was a few months ago," Julian said.

Sam disagreed. Julian was more relaxed now, and he knew a lot of that had to do with Tali, but it was more than that. Julian had found a place where he belonged. He'd been talking about the council assassins for as long as Sam could remember. He'd been in awe of them, but he was also jealous. He'd wanted to work for the council, but he'd never been contacted.

Now, he was a council assassin. He was part of that group, and it was obvious he was happy with it. Sam was still surprised Julian wanted him to help move, but also touched. He and his brother might not always see eye to eye, but they loved each other, and it was hard to think about Julian going on jobs and risking his life every day. Now that he was a council assassin, he would be better protected than he had before.

That was what Sam had to focus on. It didn't matter that he and his brother were different. They were still brothers, and he was relieved that Julian had finally found his place in life and that someone had his back.

Tony wanted to go straight to his bedroom, but it wasn't ready. He didn't care much, and he was tempted to say fuck it, but the others wouldn't want him to stay in an empty bedroom. They would insist he go back with Miles to his parents' house, something Tony wasn't sure he would be able to deal with. He'd said his goodbyes to them, and they'd already done so much for him. He wasn't leaving this warehouse any time soon, no matter what the others said.

Most of the assassins wouldn't be staying long. Today was only the day they started moving, but it was going to take a few days for everything to be here and ready for them to move in. A few were still waiting for their furniture, and Tony was one of them. His bedroom was empty except for a few boxes someone had been nice enough to get from the old warehouse, but there was no place for him to sleep or be comfortable.

He didn't care much. He wanted everyone to stop hovering over him and asking him if he was okay. He wanted them to focus on what they were doing instead of on him, but he suspected that wasn't going to happen, which was why he was hiding in the bathroom right now.

He stared at his reflection and snorted. If someone had told him he would do something like this a few months ago, he would have told them to fuck off. Instead, here he was, hiding from the people who loved him the most.

It had taken him a while to understand and accept that. In the beginning, when he'd first been contacted to become a council assassin, he'd been wary. He was a werewolf, and most shifters were afraid and prejudiced when it came to werewolves. It had taken a few of the assassins a while to warm up to him, but they'd welcomed him as if he belonged with them. And now, he did. This was his home, and they were his family. They'd accepted him being a werewolf and having powers no one else did, just like they were assuming that he was dealing with the aftermath of being tortured. They were worried about him, but then, he would be worried for any of them if they'd gone through what he'd gone through.

He was still hiding. It wasn't because of his friends, but

rather because he was overwhelmed. Part of that was their presence here. For the past few months, he'd lived only with Miles and his parents. It had been peaceful, and even then, he'd hid in his bedroom for most of the time. The warehouse was full today, though. Everyone was coming in and out, carrying boxes and furniture, laughing and talking to each other. It was a reunion after not seeing each other for a while. They were so used to sharing living space that it had been strange to be without most of them for so long. Tony ought to be out there with them, but it was too much.

The fact that he felt like he wasn't quite part of their family anymore didn't help.

It was only a feeling, and he supposed it was good to be aware of it. No one had made him feel like he didn't belong. No one had said anything about him being jumpy and acting strange. They wouldn't. They didn't care how Tony was acting as long as he was okay and that he was with them again.

No, this was all Tony. After what had happened to him, he wouldn't be able to go on a mission for a long time, if ever again. That made him feel strange. He and the others had become family because they all shared one thing—they were council assassins. They had been locked up in the labs, experimented on, and they'd come out of it different. That was one of the reasons Tony knew what was happening to him. He'd already gone through this, and he knew what PTSD looked like.

It didn't mean he was ready to deal with it.

He'd felt awful enough the first time around. He'd thought he'd left all of that behind, that he'd finally settled down into a good life. A lot of people would think that being a professional killer wasn't a good life, but Tony didn't care. The council only killed people who deserved it, people they couldn't deal with in any other way. Tony was more than happy to rid the world of people who were so evil they would take children and young adults and experiment on them. He didn't want what had happened to him to happen to anyone else.

But he wouldn't be helping with that anymore. It had been taken away from him, and he didn't know what to do with himself now. He'd been a council assassin for years. It was what he was—*who* he was. He didn't know what he could do if he couldn't be an assassin, and spending time away from all of this hadn't helped.

"Tony?"

Tony huffed. Miles had found him. He probably should have chosen another bathroom to hide in, maybe one upstairs, maybe even his own bathroom. Instead, he was downstairs in a bathroom everyone could and would use. Of course Miles had managed to find him quickly.

Tony contemplated not answering, but Miles wasn't going away. He already knew Tony was inside, and he would wait until Tony felt ready to come out, even if it happened days from now. Not that Tony could wait that long. He would have to eat sooner or later, and even though he felt the need to hide, he didn't want to.

"What?" he answered.

"Open the door."

Tony had expected this to happen, and he was kind of relieved to know it was time. "I don't need an intervention." Lately, Miles had been staring at him like he did, and maybe he wasn't wrong. Tony didn't want to talk about it, though.

"We'll call it something else. Maybe just a friendly chat?"

Tony snorted. "We both know this isn't a friendly chat."

"It's a chat with a friend, so technically, it is." Miles paused, and when he started talking again, he sounded worried. "I just want to talk to you. I promise I won't force you to leave the bathroom if you don't want to."

Tony sighed. Keeping to himself and pushing everyone

away wouldn't help. He'd done that the first time around, and he'd felt better once he'd had friends and people who cared about him. But this time was different. He couldn't help the council anymore. He was a burden, and even though his friends loved him, they wouldn't be able to deny it. Still, he didn't want to push Miles, of all people, away. Miles was his best friend, and he'd been there for Tony since they'd met. He'd supported him over the past few months, and Tony felt he owed him at least a conversation.

That was the only reason he unlocked the door. He didn't open it, but he didn't have to. Miles understood what was happening, and he stepped inside the bathroom, closing the door behind himself and locking it. He made sure to stay away from Tony, and Tony was relieved. This was already hard enough to deal with. He didn't need Miles to be in his personal space freaking him out, even though he knew that wasn't what Miles wanted.

"You're hiding," Miles said.

Tony rolled his eyes. "If that's what you wanted to talk about, you can skip it. I already know I'm hiding."

"You shouldn't be. I understand it's not as easy as saying it, but remember that we all love you and that we don't care about what happened to you. It doesn't change who you are or the fact that we care about you."

"I know." Tony truly did, but he wasn't sure it would be enough, not this time.

Sam couldn't stop looking around. When Julian had asked him for help to move into the new warehouse, he'd imagined something like the bat cave, dark and full of gadgets. Instead, this looked like any converted warehouse he'd seen in his job. Well, it was different because it hadn't been divided into several apartments. From what he'd seen, the top floor was made up of at least twenty bedrooms, each of them with a personal bathroom. The floor under that was made up of the kitchen, living room, and communal areas, while the other floors held offices, a gym, an infirmary, and under that, a garage. It was a mix of living areas and working ones, and it was interesting.

It was also something Sam wouldn't be able to sell, even if he had the opportunity. It had been set up so a large group of people could live together, which he supposed made sense in the council assassins' case, but not for a lot of other people. He might be able to sell it to some shifter group, but most of them already had places they called home. Besides, Sam wasn't supposed to sell this place. It wasn't his, and he shouldn't even know it existed. The only reason he did was because Julian lived here and trusted him, which apparently meant that the other council assassins trusted him, too. It didn't make much sense in Sam's mind, but who was he to argue?

He grabbed another box Tali had left in the shimmering room, hauled it into his arms, and headed toward the stairs. This room was next to the gym, which meant Sam and the others had to go up two flights of stairs to deposit the boxes in the bedrooms. It would have been easier if the Nix could have shimmered them where they belonged, but Sam understood why they hadn't. It was a security question, which was obviously important when it came to the council assassins.

Sam couldn't stop looking around as he walked up the stairs and through the warehouse. He knew that all the people around him were professional killers, but he was used to it. He'd grown up with both his parents and now his brother and sister doing that job. To him, it was business as usual, even though he was surprised at how the assassins behaved with each other.

They looked more like a family than like people who worked together, and they'd welcomed him as if he belonged with them. It didn't make sense, even though Julian was his brother. Julian had only recently become part of their group, and almost right away, they'd had to disband when their previous warehouse had been attacked. There was no way most of them knew Julian well enough to trust him, so why should they trust Sam?

But no one had tried to make him leave. No one had asked him what his intentions were or what he thought about them being council assassins. When Julian had introduced him, they'd waved and said hello, and that was that. It was surprising, but it helped Sam relax. They weren't the monsters he'd half expected. Julian had warned him that the council assassins worked for the council for a good reason and that they were different from normal shifters. So far, Sam hadn't noticed anything that pointed that way, but he wasn't about to ask. No matter how curious he was, it wasn't any of his business.

He was walking through the living room, headed toward the top floor, when he noticed two guys coming out of a room. He was pretty sure that was the bathroom, or at least, that was what Julian had said, and he wondered if those two were together. Sam knew that everyone here had their own bedroom, but he supposed the bathroom might be just as comfortable for a quickie, since most of the bedrooms were still empty of furniture.

For some reason, he couldn't look away. One of the guys was short and looked a bit elfish, or rather, like an elf would look like in the movies. His blond hair was cut short, but his features were long and harmonious. He might be short and slight, but Sam had no doubt he could kick Sam's ass without a second thought.

The other guy was blond, too, but that was where the similarities ended. He was tall, probably around six feet, or maybe more. His hair looked like it needed a good cut in a way that said that it wasn't supposed to look unkempt the way it did. He looked older, although, with shifters, that didn't mean much. He could be fifty or eighty. There was no way for Sam to know, but he was curious.

He was also curious about the relationship between those two. They were leaning toward each other as they talked, and it was obvious they were close. Did that mean they were just friends, or were they together? Julian had mentioned that a lot of the people who would live in the warehouse with him were mated, and those two could be part of that group.

The tall guy suddenly turned, and his gaze caught with Sam's. Sam sucked in a breath, unable to look away. The first guy was gorgeous, but this one? Sam didn't have words to describe it. Even though he looked a bit unkempt, maybe a bit too thin for his height and the amount of muscles on his body, Sam wanted to strip his clothes off and check what he was hiding under them.

Instead, he swallowed, looked away, and climbed the stairs. He didn't know why his heart was racing. It wasn't the first time a good-looking guy glanced at him, although he supposed it was the first time that good-looking guy was a professional killer. Still, Sam was used to dealing with this. It shouldn't fluster him as much as it had.

He dropped the box in Julian and Tali's bedroom. The bedroom was big enough to hold a bed, a walk-in closet, a dresser, and a small living area. The bathroom had both a shower and a bathtub, and Sam was kind of jealous. He liked his house, but he didn't have a lot of money to fix it the way he wished he could. He supposed he was lucky he'd been able to buy it at all. Julian had been moving from apartment to apartment since he'd started working, and Sam was relieved to see him finally settling down. He deserved to have a nice place to live, and he deserved to be happy with his mate.

Sam headed back downstairs, and of course, his gaze went

straight to the two guys in the corner. The shorter one was gone, although he wasn't far away, his head stuck into the fridge as he looked for something there. That left the taller and more gorgeous one alone, and Sam made a snap decision to try to talk to him.

Even as he walked toward the man, he knew this was going to be a mistake. He probably would never come back to the warehouse, even though he was Julian's brother. He didn't belong here, and he would be relieved to be away from the professional assassins. He'd tried hard not to mix his family and their jobs with the rest of his life, and that still held up. Why was he about to talk to a professional killer, then?

"Hi," he said when he reached the man. He smiled, hoping it was welcoming. "I don't think we've met. I'm Sam, Julian's brother."

The man stared at him with wide eyes. He didn't say anything, which made Sam nervous.

Sam shuffled his feet. He could go back and act as if nothing had happened, and maybe he should since he felt like an idiot. "I guess I just wanted to say hi," he murmured.

That didn't get the reaction he'd hoped for or the one he'd expected. Instead of saying hi back or telling Sam to fuck off, the guy pushed past him, knocking him against the wall. Sam just had enough time to see the guy's expression, and for some reason, he looked terrified.

Sam almost went after him, but he couldn't move, because when the guy passed by him, he got a good sniff of his scent. His stomach churned as his brain tried to process the fact that he'd just found his mate and that for some reason, the man was afraid of him.

CHAPTER TWO

Tony almost stopped. He should have, but he couldn't, not when his feet seemed to be carrying him on their own. He rushed toward the stairs, climbing them two by two until he reached his bedroom. Once there, he slammed the door behind himself and leaned against it, his heart racing so much it felt like it was about to explode.

That man, whoever he was, was Tony's mate.

Tony sucked in a breath. He had to close his eyes, but when he did, he felt like the room was twisting around him. He couldn't believe this had happened. How could he meet his mate now, when he was at his most vulnerable? How could he make such a spectacle of himself? There was no way his mate would even want to talk to him now, and Tony's stomach churned with the realization.

He'd messed things up again, and he didn't know how to fix them, or even if there was a way to do it.

A knock on the door made him jerk, and he rushed toward the corner of the room. The door was locked, though, so whoever was there couldn't come in. They tried, and when they realized they couldn't, they knocked again. "Tony? It's Miles."

"I know," Tony croaked. Everyone knew Miles was the only one Tony felt comfortable with.

"What happened? Are you okay?"

"You should go. I need some time alone."

There was a pause, and Tony knew Miles was pondering his next move. Tony wished he would just obey and fuck off, but he knew better.

He'd been in an even worse shape when he'd first come back after being tortured. He'd pushed everyone away and been rude, but Miles was still there, supporting him and being his friend. Telling him to fuck off wasn't going to work. He was worried about Tony, and that was that. He was as stubborn as they came, something for which Tony wasn't grateful right now.

"Can you tell me what happened?" Miles asked.

"I don't want to talk about it."

Miles fell silent, and Tony thought he'd won. He should have known better. It took him a moment to see what was happening, and when he did, he rushed toward the door. It was too late. Miles's arm stretched under the door and up to the lock, and he flicked open the lock.

Damn Miles's gift.

Miles stood in the hallway, victorious. He didn't hesitate to push open the door and step in, but thankfully, he closed and locked the door again behind himself. "Okay," he said as he turned around. "Let's talk about it."

Tony retreated to his corner, his arms over his chest. "I don't *want* to talk about it. And I don't like what you just did."

Miles looked unrepentant. "I wouldn't have done it if you hadn't been freaking out. I was worried about you, and I still am."

"I'm fine."

"You're not, and I would appreciate it if you stopped lying to me. What's going on? What did Sam do to you?"

Tony blinked. "Sam?"

"He introduced himself. Didn't you hear it? His name is Sam, and he's Julian's brother."

Tony sagged against the wall. He hadn't heard, probably because he'd been panicking. Now he had a name to put to his mate, but he wasn't sure how much it helped or if it changed anything.

Julian had saved Tony's life. He, Rocco, and Tali had been there for Tony when Tony had managed to escape back to the warehouse. He'd been in bad shape, and they'd healed him and protected him while the warehouse was under attack. Julian was the one who had protected Tony and the other two, and Tony would always be grateful to him for that. How could he not?

Sam wasn't Julian, though. He was Tony's mate, and he had to know, too, because if Tony had been close enough to smell Sam, the same went for Sam. There was no way for Tony to know how Sam had reacted to him running away, but he could guess it hadn't been great for him. Meeting your mate was usually a joyous experience, but this time, it had been anything but.

And it was all Tony's fault.

"Do you know Sam?" Miles asked. "Did he do anything to you? What's going on?"

Tony didn't know how to answer that. "I can't do this. I can't trust anyone I don't know, not after what happened to me."

Miles blinked, but he went along with it. "You trust *me.*"

"I already knew you from before." Tony started pacing the bedroom. "I know I can trust you because you were there before. I don't know Sam. I don't know who he is, and I don't know what he's going to do. I can't do this."

"I hear a lot of *can't.* I don't know what's going on, but I want to help. Do you know Sam?"

Tony shook his head. "This is the first time I've seen him. I hadn't even caught his name or who he was. But there's no way I can do this. I'm vulnerable enough as it is. I'm broken, helpless, and there's no way he's going to want me."

Miles's eyes widened. "Want you as in being your boyfriend?"

Right. Miles didn't know that Sam and Tony were mates. Tony didn't want to tell him, but he also did. He was confused, but then, when wasn't he confused? Once he'd come back from being tortured, he felt like he didn't know anything anymore.

He stopped in front of Miles. He didn't look at him—he didn't think he could—but he forced the words out of his mouth. "He's my mate. That's what I mean." Then he started moving again. "And there's no way he's going to want to talk to me after the way I reacted to his presence."

"Did you run away because he's your mate?" Miles asked cautiously.

"No. I was already leaving when I smelled him, but I couldn't stop. I panicked when he came up to me and introduced himself, because I didn't know him." Or at least, that was what Miles said Sam had done. Tony hadn't heard him, and now, he wished he had. He didn't even know the sound of Sam's voice.

"So you panicked because he's someone new, and you don't know if you can trust him. That's understandable."

Tony stopped again. "It's not. If this had happened to me a year ago, I would have smiled at him and introduced myself. I would have been happy to meet him." But he couldn't be, not when his entire world was on fire, not when he wasn't the same man he'd been before he'd been tortured.

Dammit. He hated this situation. He hated that he was so weak that being tortured had this impact on him. He'd already been through so much, even worse than what had been done to him recently. Why had things gone so badly?

Miles raised his hands, maybe to try to placate Tony. "I understand. Things are different now, and no matter how much you hate it, you're going to have to roll with it."

"How can I? I can't even talk to my own mate because I don't trust him. I'm *afraid* of him and of everyone new in my

21

life. Why do you think I've been hiding in your parents' guestroom? I was ashamed, but I couldn't face them, not when I panicked every time one of them looked at me. I *knew* I could trust them, but I still couldn't. Why would Sam agree to be with someone like that? Why would he want to talk to me when I'm broken and afraid to be touched? He's not just someone else. He's my mate, and he's going to want to be with me as one. I can't give him that."

Tony wished he could. He wanted to be healed, to be able to forget everything about the torture, but he couldn't. He saw it, again and again, every time he closed his eyes, and it was too much to ask for Sam to deal with it. Tony never wanted to be a burden, and he already was one when it came to Miles and the other assassins. He couldn't drag Sam into this, too.

He couldn't give Sam anything. He was broken, and as far as he was concerned, he couldn't be fixed. He'd been trying for the past few months, but nothing had worked. Maybe he would get better in time, but he couldn't ask Sam to wait for him.

This was one more thing the people who had tortured him were taking from him. They weren't happy with torturing him and getting the location of the warehouse out of him. They had to ruin his life, and they'd managed. Even though they didn't know about it, Tony did, and it made him want to hunt those people down and torture them the way they had tortured him.

Sam had no idea what had just happened. He'd introduced himself just like he did every day for his job, with a smile and an offered hand. The guy he now knew was his mate had looked at him as if he expected Miles to beat him up, and he'd run away. The other guy, the smallest one, had gone after him with wide eyes, leaving Sam standing there with no clue what to do.

His cheeks felt warm, and he looked around, wondering if anyone had noticed what had just happened. Julian had — because of course he had — but as far as Sam could see, he was the only one.

And he couldn't just let this go.

"What did you do?" he asked when he reached Sam.

"I didn't do anything."

"That's not what it looked like. Did you say anything rude?"

Sam glared at him. "Since when am I rude with people I don't know?"

Julian cocked his head as he watched Sam. "Okay, you're not wrong there. Maybe you're just so ugly that Tony couldn't bear to look at you."

Sam groaned and pinched the bridge of his nose. "Now isn't the moment to tease me." Because whatever had happened, that man was Sam's mate, and Sam had to do something about it. He didn't know what, but he would find out.

Since Julian lived here and knew these people, Sam turned to him. "What's his name?"

Julian frowned. "Whose name?"

"The guy who ran away, the first one. What's his name?"

"You mean the tall one? That was Tony, and the other one was Miles."

"Are they together?"

"They're not a couple if that's what you're asking. They're best friends."

Sam relaxed. It wasn't much, but at least he wouldn't have to deal with a boyfriend. "Do you know if Tony has anyone in his life?"

"I have no idea why you're asking all these questions, but I'm going to ignore that and answer because I'm curious. No, as far as I know, Tony doesn't have anyone." Julian hesitated, which meant something was wrong. "Something happened to him a few months ago, when the warehouse was attacked. That might be why he ran away."

"*What* happened?"

"I don't know if I can tell you. I want to," he added when Sam's frown deepened. "But it's not my story to tell."

"I need to know. Please. I didn't do anything to him except for introducing myself, and I'm worried."

"I can see that. I just don't understand *why* you're so worried."

Sam didn't know if he should answer. Julian would be happy for him if he told him Tony was his mate, and it might be the only way for Sam to get the whole story. He felt guilty about insisting, and Tony might get angry when he found out. Would he blame Sam? Sam wanted to know why his mate had run away from him.

It wasn't like Julian wouldn't find out sooner or later, so Sam decided to tell him. He looked around, making sure no one was hovering around. They were a few people in the room, and they were looking curiously at Sam, but thankfully, they kept their distance. Still, Sam leaned closer to Julian so only he would hear him. "The tall guy, Tony?"

Julian rolled his eyes. "I know who Tony is. I just told you."

"What you don't know is that he's my mate."

Julian stared at Sam with wide eyes. "Are you serious?"

"I wouldn't joke about something like that. I'm serious, yes. Tony *is* my mate, and I have no idea what to do now."

Julian reached out and squeezed Sam's shoulder. "I'm happy for you."

"Sure you are."

"I am. Both for you and for Tony. This isn't going to be easy, though."

Sam shrugged Julian's hand off. "I don't care. Would you have left and ignored Tali if he'd done what Tony just did? If something was wrong with him? If you knew that being with him wouldn't be easy?"

"I wouldn't have. I shouldn't have suggested it, and I'm sorry."

Sam was pretty sure he'd heard that wrong. "You just admitted I was right?"

"I did, but I won't make a habit, so you should savor the moment." Julian looked around, too. "All right, I'm going to tell you what happened to Tony, but that's only because you're his mate and you deserve to know what you're up against. I don't know him well, but he was a nice guy before this happened to him. He definitely wouldn't have run when he met you."

Sam supposed it was a relief, although not a big one. Whatever Tony would or wouldn't have done before, it wasn't what he'd done today.

Julian steered Sam toward the wide window seat. They both sat down, Sam looking out the window. Whatever Julian was about to say, he knew it wouldn't be easy to listen to it.

"So you know the old warehouse where the council assassins lived was attacked a few months ago," Julian started.

"I do. You told us about it, remember? That's why you're moving here."

Julian nodded. "Exactly. The warehouse was attacked, which means it wasn't safe anymore. It had been before because it had a great security system, and no one knew it was there. Someone managed to find its position, which is why they knew where to attack." Julian sucked in a breath. "And the reason they knew where the warehouse was is that they captured Tony and tortured the information out of him."

Sam felt numb. He'd expected something like this, but now that he'd heard the words, he didn't know what to do with them.

He was a real estate agent. He didn't deal with assassins,

with people being tortured. This wasn't his life.

Except that now, it was.

Whatever Tony was, whatever had happened to him, it wouldn't be enough to push Sam away. He wanted to do something for Tony, to help him, but how? "That's why he ran away just now?" he asked.

"When Tony managed to escape, he was in bad shape. He got here just before the attack, but it was enough to warn us, and we managed to defend ourselves. We had a few wounded, but no one was badly hurt, and it's thanks to him. What they did to him changed him, though. It took weeks for him to heal, even with our Nix healers, and his behavior changed."

Sam didn't know anything about being tortured, but he thought he knew what Julian was talking about. "PTSD?"

Julian shrugged. "I'm not a doctor. I can't confirm or deny that. But yes, my guess is that he has PTSD."

How could Sam help with that? He might know the word, but he had no idea what it meant. Even with his strange family, he'd never had to deal with anything like that.

"Unfortunately, I can't tell you much more about Tony," Julian continued. "He was in Gillham for a while, but as soon as he was fine physically, he left. From what I know, he stayed with Miles and Miles's parents. I don't know what happened while he was there. Obviously, he's still dealing with all of this, and who could blame him?"

Where did that leave Sam? He wanted to at least talk to Tony, but obviously, he wouldn't be able to. The last thing he wanted was to push Tony to do something that made him uncomfortable, or worse, that sent him into another panic.

They were mates, though. That had to mean something. It did for Sam, but maybe it wouldn't be enough for Tony. Sam didn't expect Tony to get over his PTSD and for everything to be perfect in their lives suddenly, but he wanted to be there for his mate. He wouldn't be able to do that if Tony refused to talk to him, but he had no idea how to deal with someone with PTSD. Should he try talking to Tony, or should he give his mate space and allow Tony to move at his own pace? He wanted to talk to Tony and reassure him, but doing that could easily make things worse, and that was the last thing Sam wanted.

Whatever happened next, he felt it would be crucial to their future relationship. The problem was that he had no idea what to do or how to behave.

"I think that the first thing you need to do is to calm down," Miles said.

He sounded reasonable, and Tony wanted to do what he was suggesting. He didn't think he could, though. "*How* am I supposed to calm down?"

Miles came closer and reached out to touch Tony's shoulders.

That was enough to make Tony freeze. He knew Miles wouldn't hurt him, but his first and only instinct was to run away and hide. Instead, he swallowed and forced himself to look at his best friend.

Tony couldn't power through PTSD. That wasn't how it worked, no matter how much he wished it did. But this was Miles. He was the guy who had been there when Tony had still been healing. He was the guy who had offered Tony a place to stay and who'd made sure Tony was safe and as happy as he could be once he was there. He'd been by Tony's side for the past few months, and if there was one person Tony could trust, it was him.

Tony tried to relax his shoulders. He wasn't sure he could, but he was breathing faster. Thankfully, Miles seemed to notice, and he let go. Tony breathed easier once he did.

"I'm sorry I did that," Miles said. "I know you don't like being touched, and I shouldn't have."

Tony shook his head. "I don't think I would have stopped freaking out if you hadn't. Thank you."

Miles grimaced. "Don't thank me for freaking you out so much that you snapped out of your loop. But anyway. Now that you can breathe easier, we can talk about Sam."

Tony stepped away. His back hit the wall, which meant he couldn't go any further. In times like these, he wished he was a small shifter like Miles, or maybe Julian. If he shifted into a rabbit, he would be able to hide somewhere. Instead, his shifted form was fucking huge, which meant it would be better for him to stay in his human one.

Miles's expression twisted, but he stayed where he was. His hands were still raised as if trying to make himself look harmless. Tony already knew he was, but it was hard to convince his brain of that. He took a deep breath, then another. Once he felt calmer, he looked at his best friend again. "Okay. Let's talk about it."

Miles's looked surprised, but he nodded. "First things first. I'm happy you found your mate. You of all people deserve happiness, and I hope he'll be able to give you that."

Tony grimaced. "I wouldn't count on it. You saw how I reacted. I didn't even stop to talk to him. He has to think I'm a freak."

"I doubt that. Besides, he's Julian's brother. I'm pretty sure Julian is telling him what happened to you right now."

The thought should have made Tony angry. That was his story to tell, but he knew himself. He wouldn't have been able to look at Sam in the eyes and tell him what had been done to him and what it had left him as. He didn't think he would thank Julian for doing it for him, but he was relieved. "So he's going to know how broken I am."

"God, I really want to touch you right now, but I'm not sure if it's to hug you or slap you."

Tony grinned for what felt like the first time in forever. This was one of the reasons he loved Miles. "You could do both."

"I would if I weren't afraid of freaking you out. But you're not broken, Tony. You went through something awful, not once, but twice, the second time only a few months ago. I know that to you, it has to feel like an eternity and like it's never going to end, but you have to give yourself time to heal."

"I *am* healed." But that didn't mean he wasn't broken, at least inside.

"Physically, sure. Mentally, though, that's nowhere near true. I know you don't want to talk about this, though, so I'm going to focus on Sam for a moment, okay?"

Tony swallowed. "I'm listening." Because if there was one person who could talk some sense into him, it was Miles.

"I don't know Sam. I've never talked to him, so I can't make any promises. I *do* know Julian, though, and if Sam is anything like him, he'll understand. Julian was there when you came back. He knows what you went through, both when you were tortured and when you arrived back here. He protected you, and I'm pretty sure he's going to do it again if he has to."

"Not against his brother."

"I don't think his brother is going to attack and torture you. But Julian is protective of you. You know how many times he called me to make sure you were okay while we were at my parents' house? At least once a day."

"Really?" Tony hadn't known. When he'd arrived there, he'd told Miles he didn't want to talk to anyone. He'd missed his friends—his family—but he didn't want any of them to see how weak he was. He knew all of them had called Miles at one time or another, but he was surprised to find out that Julian had called every day.

"Really. There's no way Sam is a bad person. He might not

know how to deal with what happened to you, but he's not going to hold it against you."

Miles couldn't know that for sure, but what could Tony say? He didn't want Miles to worry about him any more than he already was. "I'll be fine," he said.

Miles's snorted. "Who are you trying to convince? You or me? Because I'm pretty sure neither of us actually believes that."

"Something has to happen. I can't ignore Sam, not when I'm pretty sure he knows I'm his mate. He's going to want at least to talk to me." But Tony didn't know if he could do that.

Miles was okay, and so were all the other people Tony had lived with and trusted before he'd been tortured. Sam was new, though. There was no way for Tony to know what he was going to do or say, or if he could trust him.

But Sam was his mate. If Tony couldn't trust him, could he truly trust anyone else?

This was a mess, and Tony didn't know what to do with it. He was calmer now. It was easier to think, and he realized how badly he'd treated Sam. Hopefully, Sam would understand. If he didn't, Tony supposed it would give him his answer as to whether or not he should trust his mate.

"I want you to talk to him," he told Miles.

"You want *me* to talk to Sam?" Miles asked as if making sure he'd heard Tony right.

"Please. I can't go downstairs right now. I'd freak out again, and it's the last thing I want to happen. But I trust you. I know that you'll treat him right and that you'll be able to say whether or not I should trust him."

Miles grimaced. "That's a lot you're putting on my shoulders."

"Maybe, and I apologize. There's no one I trust more than you, though. If you think I should talk to Sam after you've talked to him, I will."

"That's not how it's supposed to happen."

"None of this is how it's supposed to happen, but I don't have a choice. I should talk to him because he's my mate, and I treated him badly. But I can't do that unless I know I can trust him not to hurt me."

"I'll go talk to him, but I'm not making any promises."

"That's fine." It had to be. There was nothing else Tony could do. If he went downstairs to talk to Sam right now, he would break down even worse than he had already. No one wanted that to happen, but especially not Tony, and not in front of his mate.

He didn't know if he would ever trust Sam or talk to him, but he needed to try. He owed it to Sam—and to himself.

Sam kept peeking at the stairs. Now that he knew what Tony had gone through, he wanted to talk to him even more, but he knew better than to try.

He didn't know how to reassure Tony that he didn't care what had happened to him or what wounds it had left in him. This wasn't going to be easy, but Sam wasn't afraid of hard work. He would do whatever Tony was comfortable with and whatever he needed, but first, he had to talk to him.

Instead, he stayed downstairs. Tony had panicked, and Sam didn't want to make it worse. It would be a disaster, and it would push his mate even further away from him. If Sam had one chance to make something happen with Tony, he needed to be careful about what he did and said.

He almost dropped the box he was holding when Miles came down the stairs. He now knew that Miles was Tony's best friend, and Miles had been upstairs with Tony, talking to him until now. That meant he probably knew what was happening, and hopefully, he was here to talk to Sam.

Sam put the box onto the nearest flat surface and waited.

He was relieved when Miles came toward him, but also nervous.

"I'm Miles," Miles said when he reached Sam.

Sam offered him his hand, and Miles shook it. "I'm Sam, Julian's brother."

Miles's smiled. "I got that the first time you introduced yourself. It's a pleasure to meet you."

"The same goes for me, although I wish things had been different."

Miles dropped Sam's hand and grimaced. "Same. Did Julian talk to you?"

"He told me what happened to Tony after I told him Tony is my mate."

Miles didn't look surprised, so Sam guessed that Tony had told him while they were talking upstairs. "Good. I wasn't looking forward to going over all of that once more."

Sam gestured at the window seat. This wasn't his home, but he felt like he and Miles needed some space and quiet away from the people who were walking in and out of the room. It would be better if they could close themselves in a room to talk, but this was better than nothing.

Miles grinned and flopped onto the window seat. He peeked outside, his expression a strange mix of wistfulness and happiness. "You know what happened to the old warehouse, then," he started.

"I already knew it had been attacked, but now I know how it was found, too." He hesitated. He didn't want to sound like he was demanding, not when it was in his right to know. "How is he?"

"As well as you can imagine."

"Did he freak out because I came too close or because I'm his mate?"

Miles's eyebrows rose on his forehead. "I'm surprised you think there's a difference."

"I hope there is. If he freaked out because I came too close, I'm hoping there's a way to change that. If it's because I'm his mate, though, it will be harder."

Miles nodded. "You're right. It's the first one. He doesn't like being touched by anyone, and that includes me. That's not all of it, though. Tony has had a hard time, even with the people he already knows and trusts. You're an unknown entity, and he doesn't know if he can trust you, even though you're his mate. You're new in his life, and it's not going to be easy for him to open up to you, especially considering the wounds he still bears from the torture."

"Do you mean physical wounds?" Because Julian had said Tony had been healed, so Sam hoped that wasn't the case.

"I wish. Those would be easier to heal, but it's not what I'm talking about."

"He has PTSD."

Miles nodded. "Probably, although he won't talk to anyone about it. We recognize it, though. I'm sure Julian already told you why everyone here was contacted by the council and asked to work for them."

Sam hadn't known until Julian had explained, and he doubted Julian had known until he'd become part of their group. "Because you were all tortured and *changed* in those labs."

"Exactly. We all went through that. We know what torture is and what wounds it can leave behind. It took us a long time to deal with it, and the fact that Tony has to do it twice is unimaginable. I want to help him, but he won't let me in, even though I'm his best friend. Frankly, I'm hoping that the fact that you're his mate will help, but I can't make any promises, and I don't think he can, either. If you want anything to happen with him, even if it's only to get to know him, you're going to have to give him space and time."

Sam wasn't sure what he wanted. He'd barely met Tony,

and all of this was new. What he did know was that he wouldn't give up Tony without at least trying, no matter how hard it was. "I'm more than ready to do that."

Miles stared at him for a moment before nodding. He looked satisfied, and Sam felt like he'd passed the test he hadn't known he was taking. "Good. Tony has a big family, as you can see. We're also pretty dangerous. There's going to be a line to kick your ass if you hurt him intentionally."

Sam swallowed. "I'm pretty sure you're going to have to wait behind my brother. He's really protective of Tony."

"He has a right to be. He's the one who defended Tony and the people helping him when he escaped after being tortured. He kept the assholes who attacked us away long enough that his mate was able to shimmer them away to safety."

For all that Julian seemed to be empty-headed sometimes, he really wasn't. He was an extremely caring person, which didn't make sense, considering his job. Sam had stopped trying to understand his brother a long time ago.

"I'll respect Tony's wishes," Sam said slowly, trying to think about how they could move this forward without hurting Tony or himself. "Can I give you my phone number?"

"Of course. I suppose I should have it, considering you're my best friend's mate."

"There's that, but I also hope you can give it to Tony if he wants it."

Miles's smile fell a bit. "I wish I didn't have to say this, but I don't want you to get hurt any more than I want Tony to be. I wouldn't expect too much, if I were you. He's having a hard time, and while meeting his mate would have made him happy at any other time in his life, he's a mess right now. He thinks he's weak and broken, and he doesn't want you to have to deal with that. There's also the fact that he can't trust new people, which doesn't help."

"Just give him my number. He can use it or not, and either

way will be fine. But I want him to have a way to get to know me without actually being in the same room as me. You said he can't trust me because he doesn't know me. Isn't this the best way for him to actually get to know me without freaking out?"

Miles stared at Sam for a moment before nodding. "You might be right. You know, I think I'm going to like you."

"Are you?"

"You're not giving up on him, are you? Even though it's going to be hard and it would be easier for you to forget about him, you won't do that."

"I'm not ready to give up without trying. I can't make any promises, but I'm going to try." It was all he could do, both for himself and for Tony. Hopefully, it would be enough.

He didn't know what he would do if it wasn't, but he prayed he wouldn't have to find out.

CHAPTER THREE

Tony unlocked his phone, brought up his contacts, and scrolled down until he got to Sam's name. Then he locked the phone again and put it down on the bed. He couldn't stop looking at it, though, no matter how hard he tried.

He huffed and rolled to his back, staring at the ceiling.

He was lucky his furniture had arrived. That meant he was finally staying in his new bedroom in the warehouse that was now his home, and he felt more relaxed. It still didn't quite feel like his yet, mostly because he hadn't brought a lot of his things from the old warehouse, but he knew that would change.

If he stayed with the council assassins.

He didn't want to leave. They were his family, and he was used to living with them. He didn't want to lose that, or any of them. He didn't think he could be a council assassin anymore, though. He couldn't even leave his bedroom. How could he go on a mission on his own to kill someone and make it back in one piece? His last mission had been a disaster, and he was still living with the consequences of that.

But no one had asked him to leave. He hadn't seen anyone but Miles since his furniture had arrived and he'd locked himself into his bedroom, but he could hear the others moving around the house, and it was soothing in a way he hadn't expected. No one had pushed to talk to him, even though from what Miles said, they were worried. They were giving him all the time and space he needed, and he was grateful.

Which brought him back to Sam. For now, the rest of

Tony's life was settled. He was in his new bedroom, and he wasn't going to be asked to leave. He was safe, or at least, as safe as he could be considering the kind of job he'd done until recently. Sam, on the other hand, was an unknown entity in Tony's life.

Sometimes Tony wished he could just forget about Sam, act as if his mate didn't exist. It shouldn't have been as hard as it was, but he couldn't deny that his thoughts kept going back to Sam. Tony's werewolf grumbled unhappily in the back of Tony's mind. The beast wanted to go to their mate, and it wasn't afraid of Sam the way Tony's human side was. It didn't understand why Tony was acting like this, and sometimes, neither did Tony.

He trusted Miles and everyone else in the house. Why couldn't he trust Sam, who was his mate and the one person in the world who was made for him?

Tony knew the answer to that. He couldn't trust Sam because he didn't know him. He couldn't be a hundred percent sure that Sam wouldn't hurt him the way the people who had caught him during his last mission had. He was pretty sure Sam wouldn't torture him, but that wasn't the only way to hurt someone.

Besides, maybe Sam wouldn't want to be anywhere close to Tony. After all, Tony was broken and helpless, and he couldn't let anyone touch him. Every time someone did, he had flashbacks to when he'd been tortured. What could Tony offer Sam? They were mates, but they wouldn't be able to touch each other. They could have conversations, but that couldn't be enough. Sam seemed to be a good person, and he deserved so much more than what Tony could give him.

Tony rolled to his stomach again and stared at his phone. He knew Sam deserved so much more and that he should keep his distance, but he also wanted to get to know Sam. He couldn't trust Sam now, but maybe he would be different.

Since he was Tony's mate, it was possible that eventually, Tony could allow him to touch him. Tony didn't want to give that up, not when he missed being hugged and loved. He missed human touch, and he was pretty sure Sam was the only one who could give him that — but only if Tony allowed him to.

And God, how much he wanted to allow him to. Tony despised feeling like there were two people inside of him — the Tony from before, who wanted to get to know Sam, kiss him, and bond with him, and the Tony who had been tortured and needed to keep his distance from everyone unless he wanted to freak out. Tony never quite knew which Tony was the real one, and it made everything more complicated.

He snatched his phone from the bed and sat up. He could do this. After all, Sam didn't expect anything from him. He'd given his phone number to Miles in the hope that Tony would use it, but so far, Tony hadn't. He'd been too afraid, and he still was, but this was kind of perfect, which pointed to the fact that Sam understood Tony better than Tony had expected anyone could. He knew Tony wouldn't be able to stand being in the same room as him or to talk face to face, but this was different. There was a screen between them, and Tony hoped it would help him be himself instead of the Tony he'd been since the torture.

There was only one way to find out.

He unlocked the phone, clicked on Sam's number, and typed a message.

Hi. It's Tony.

He sent it, and of course, regretted it only seconds later. His heart raced as he stared at the screen, wondering what was going to happen. Sam couldn't hurt him, not through the phone, but Tony was making himself vulnerable in a way he never wanted to be again. Could he truly do this?

The phone vibrated in Tony's hand, and he almost threw it against the wall in surprise. He dropped it on the bed instead, then scrambled to snatch it again, needing to see what Sam was texting him.

Hi. I'm glad you used my number.

Tony hadn't expected much, but it made him smile. He wanted to answer. Sam deserved for him to answer.

He had no idea what to say, though.

That didn't seem to be a problem for Sam, who was already texting again. *I wasn't sure you would when I gave it to Miles. He told me that you probably wouldn't, which I admit I found kind of disappointing.*

Tony never wanted to disappoint anyone, but that was his life now.

So I'm glad you texted me. Feel free to ignore my texts if you're overwhelmed or if you don't want to talk to me, and tell me if you want me to stop.

Tony chuckled. The sound was rough and sounded odd to Tony's ears. It had been a while since he'd last laughed.

If only Sam knew that Tony never wanted him to stop texting. He realized it wasn't a balanced relationship. Sam was reaching out to him, and he should do the same.

He couldn't. The thought of opening himself up that way made his stomach churn, and it made him want to run away. He couldn't run away from his phone, but he *could* avoid answering.

So he did. He stayed on his bed, staring at the phone. Sam continued texting throughout the day. It was never anything important, but he told Tony what he was eating at lunch, he mentioned the TV series he was enjoying right now, and he told Tony about the kind of books he liked to read.

It was odd, but in the best of ways. It made Tony feel connected to him, even though he wasn't answering or telling Sam about himself. It gave him hope because if Sam wasn't giving up now, maybe he would be strong enough to stand by Tony's side while Tony tried to put order in his life.

Sam wouldn't be able to make any promises, and Tony

didn't expect anything from him. He understood that being with him, even only as his friend, was overwhelming and hard. Miles hadn't complained, but then, he never did. The fact that Sam was still texting even though Tony hadn't answered made Tony's heart flutter in the best of ways. It wasn't fear, or at least, not only fear. There was also hope.

It was a lot to put on Sam's shoulders, and Tony knew he couldn't start healing just for Sam. Still, knowing that Sam was in his life gave him a reason to. He'd been isolating himself, afraid of getting hurt, and he hadn't realized that he was hurting himself that way. There would be no miracle, but maybe texting Sam was the first step for Tony to heal from the torture and the consequences it had left in his life and mind.

Even though Tony never answered any of Sam's texts, Sam was happy. He and Tony were making progress.

It wouldn't seem like a lot to anyone else, and Sam could admit it wasn't. In any other relationship, he would be offended that the person he was texting was reading his messages but not answering. Now that he knew about Tony and what he'd gone through, though, he understood that Tony reaching out was huge. He'd manage to get over his fear of Sam and not knowing him.

So Sam kept texting Tony through the day, making sure to tell him about himself. It wasn't much, just his likes and dislikes, but it was the first step, and hopefully, it would be followed by many others.

And it gave him something that wasn't his job to focus on.

Sometimes Sam wondered what he'd been thinking when he'd decided to become a real estate agent. Then he remembered, and he cursed himself for wanting to be different and for going about it this way.

Growing up in the house he'd grown up in and with the

family he had, his life had been strange, to say the least. His mother had been a stay-at-home mom, but his father had continued working as a professional killer. It made for odd conversations with Sam's school friends. Sam had never been able to tell anyone what his father did, and he'd never wanted to. It had made him feel different, though. He couldn't invite anyone to his house for the afternoon, because what if his father had his gun on the kitchen table? It had kept him apart, and even today, he had a hard time making friends.

His father's job was the main reason that had pushed Sam the way he'd gone in life. His parents had never expected any of their children to step into their shoes, but both of Sam's siblings had. Sam had never understood how they could, especially considering the kind of life they'd had. Neither Julian nor Kara had hesitated, though. They both worked as professional killers now, just like their father, and probably their mother again soon.

Then there was Sam, the real estate agent.

He still wasn't sure why he'd chosen that job. Sam liked taking care of people, so he supposed it kind of made sense, but not a lot. He enjoyed the part where he had to help people find their forever home, but he hated everything else about the job—the unsteady hours, the feeling that he always needed to work because if he didn't, he wouldn't earn enough money to get through the month. He disliked having to interact with some of the people he found homes for. Most of them were nice, but some were rude and demanding, and they were the worst kind of clients.

So no, he didn't like his job, but he still forced himself to smile through the day as he set up an open house and welcomed visitors. His mind was mostly on Tony, which helped.

Sam had always disliked the professional assassin profession, and now, his own mate was one. It was hard to wrap his mind around, but he had to come to terms with it and stop obsessing over being normal if he wanted any kind of chance with Tony. It was a complication Tony didn't need to deal with and that he probably *couldn't* deal with. He already had enough problems as it was. Sam couldn't add more of them, especially not personal problems that were only his.

He was startled when his phone rang. He half hoped it was Tony, even though he knew it couldn't be. Tony wasn't even answering his texts. There was no way he was going to call to talk to him. Sure enough, it was Julian, and Sam was tempted not to answer. His brother no doubt wanted to know what was going on between Sam and Tony, and Sam didn't have an answer for him. He wasn't sure if Julian would tease him or understand. In any other situation, Julian would annoy the fuck out of Sam, but this wasn't a normal circumstance. Julian was protective of Tony, and he'd understand why Tony wasn't answering Sam's texts.

With a sigh, Sam answered. "I'm working."

"Do I sound like I care?" Julian asked.

Sam had to suppress a laugh. He couldn't show Julian how amused he was because Julian wouldn't stop calling him at work if he did that. The last thing Julian needed was to be encouraged. "I already know you don't. What do you want?"

"To tell you I love you."

Sam snorted so loudly that one of the people looking at the house turned to glance at him. He smiled at the woman, then turned his attention back to Julian. "We both know that's a lie. I'm pretty sure you tried to strangle me when I was a child."

"Only because you wouldn't stop crying. Anyway, I wanted to ask if you wanted to come over."

Sam blinked. "Come over where?" He was pretty sure Julian and his mate had moved into the new warehouse by now. There was no way Julian was asking him to visit there, though, right?

"The place I live? You know, the huge warehouse you

visited the other day."

"I wasn't sure you'd want to see me there again. Are your friends okay with my presence?"

There was a pause before Julian asked, "Are you serious right now?"

"I wouldn't be asking if I weren't."

"No one cares about you."

Sam smiled again. "Thank you. That's soothing to my ego."

"You know what I mean. Did anyone say something to you when you were here? Were they rude to you?"

"*You* were, but then, I suppose that's normal."

"As far as I saw, everyone welcomed you, and they didn't care about your presence. They trust you."

And Sam didn't understand why. He'd only met most of these people once. Hell, he barely even knew his brother's mate. Why would they welcome him the way they had? Why would it be normal for them to see Sam walking around the warehouse when he wasn't an assassin or a mate to one?

"Anyway, I already asked Win, and he's okay with you coming for dinner."

"Why?"

"Because you're my brother, and I vouched for you."

That made Sam feel warm inside, something he didn't usually associate with Julian. "I don't understand why they trust me."

"Because you're my brother, and I vouched for you," Julian slowly repeated, as if he thought Sam was an idiot.

Sam huffed. "Fine. I don't understand why they would trust you like that, but I suppose they know what they're doing. Why do *you* want me to come over for dinner, though?" Sam had always kept himself separate from Julian's professional life. Of course, he'd never actually had the opportunity to mix with it. As far as he knew, Julian had never been best friends with any of the other professional assassins he'd worked against.

The council assassins were different. They didn't work against each other, but rather, together.

"Because you need to be comfortable with everyone."

Sam hadn't expected that, either. How was Julian still surprising him after so many years? "What do you mean?"

"You're Tony's mate. Unless you decide to reject him, you're going to spend a lot of time around here."

"He barely talks to me."

"For now. You're both shifters, though, which gives you years to get used to the situation."

That much was true, although Sam hoped it wouldn't take Tony years to talk to him. He wasn't sure he could continue texting into the void the way he'd been since this morning. "Are you trying to play matchmaker?"

Julian laughed. "I don't need to play matchmaker. You and Tony are already mates. You just need an opportunity to get together and fall in love. I never said it was going to be easy, but since it is what it is, you might as well become comfortable with all the other assassins and with the warehouse. You'll move here eventually if you and Tony get together, and I know how uncomfortable you are with what we do. I guess I'm asking you to come for dinner to give us a chance to show you we're not monsters."

Sam swallowed painfully. Was that really what Julian thought? That Sam viewed him and Kara and their parents as monsters? If he did, it was all Sam's fault, and he needed to change that. He might never understand why his family wanted to do this job, but that didn't mean he didn't love them or that he thought they were monsters.

When someone knocked on Tony's door, he glared at it. It could only be one person, and he wasn't sure he wanted to talk to Miles, but Miles would get worried if Tony didn't at least answer, so he called out, "Yes?"

"Sam is here."

Tony already knew that. Sam had texted him that Julian had invited him over for dinner. He'd asked Tony if it would be okay with him if he came, but Tony hadn't been able to answer. He wanted to, but it was as if he couldn't make his fingers move. So Sam had told him that he *would* be coming, and Tony only had to ask him to leave if he didn't want to see him. That wasn't going to be a problem, since Tony wasn't planning on leaving his bedroom. He wanted to see Sam, but he was also terrified to see him.

Sam knew what had happened to Tony. He knew how weak Tony was, which meant he knew all the bad things about Tony and only that. Why would he want to be with Tony or even to talk to him?

"Tony?" Miles called out again.

Tony huffed. "I heard you, and I already knew he was coming. There's no need for you to tell me."

"How did you know?"

"He texted me."

Tony was pretty sure Miles was vibrating with the need to ask how Sam had gotten Tony's number. Thankfully, he didn't.

"What do you want to do?" Miles asked instead.

"Nothing. What am I supposed to do?"

"You could come downstairs to talk to him."

Tony snorted. They both knew there was a fat chance of that happening. "I'll be staying here. Thanks for reaching out, though."

Miles laughed. "You sound like an asshole. You know, it would be much easier to talk if I could come into your room."

"I know." But Tony didn't get up from the bed to open the door. He didn't think he had the strength to do it, not after the day he'd had.

To anyone else, having your mate text you time and time again would be nothing. To Tony, it was everything, and while he was grateful that Sam wasn't giving up on him, he also needed time to wrap his mind around all of it, including what he wanted or didn't want to do in the future.

He didn't want to make himself vulnerable, but he also wanted to see Sam. Those two things didn't work together, but maybe there was a way for them to mesh. After all, Sam had managed to allow Tony to get to know him, even though Tony had pretty much ignored him.

It wasn't fair to Sam. Tony wouldn't go as far as saying that Sam deserved another mate, because he didn't want to give him or the bond up, but he had to make an effort. This was already complicated enough with Tony not being able to touch Sam or to allow Sam to touch him. The least Tony could do was try to talk to Sam and see him in person.

They hadn't done that since the day they'd met, and Tony wished he'd gotten a better look at Sam when he'd had the chance. He knew that Sam looked a bit like Julian, which made sense, since they were brothers. He had brown hair and possibly brown eyes. He was also about Julian's height, but Tony didn't want to continue comparing Sam to Julian. He wanted to see him for himself, which wouldn't happen until he *actually* saw him. The only way to do that was to leave his bedroom, and Tony wasn't ready for that. He didn't think he ever would be, or at least, it felt like it.

"I know this is hard," Miles's said softly.

Tony snorted. "You don't. We all went through something similar after we were released from the labs, but none of us found our mate during that time. You don't know how hard it is to want to see Sam and talk to him but not be able to. It's a war I fight against myself, and it feels like it's never going to end or to get better. I want everything with Sam, but I can't even answer his texts. How is that fair?"

"It's not, to you or Sam. It's not your fault, though. You're doing your best with what you have and what was done to you, and Sam knows that. He understands."

"For how long? He wants a mate, and he deserves one. He shouldn't have to deal with my problems, not when even *I* don't want to deal with them."

Miles huffed. Tony understood it was frustrating to talk to him about this. He should probably see a professional, something Miles had suggested more than once, but he couldn't bring himself to do it. It was bad enough that everyone here knew what had happened to him and could see how badly he was taking it. He didn't need more people to be aware of it. Besides, he already knew that talking about what was done to him wouldn't help. It would still take years for him to get over it, and he felt like he didn't have those years. He needed to do something more drastic, but what?

There was no way to work around this or rush it. There was no way for him to go back to the man he'd been before and give Sam a fair chance.

"How about Sam comes up here?" Miles said.

Tony was pretty sure he'd missed part of the conversation, but he wasn't about to ask Miles to repeat himself. "What do you mean?"

"You two could talk the way you and I are talking."

And Tony still wouldn't be able to see Sam. He didn't know why, but it was important to him and his werewolf. The beast was pushing at him to open the door and go downstairs, grab their mate and possibly drag him back upstairs, but just the thought of doing that made Tony freeze in terror.

"Or you could open the door," Miles continued. "He wouldn't come in if you told him not to."

"It would be his right to."

"No, it wouldn't be. This isn't his home, and it's not his

bedroom. No one will come in unless you invite them to, and that includes Sam. I already warned him that you have a lot of people who care about you and who won't hesitate to hurt him if he does anything to you."

Tony groaned. "I can't believe you had that conversation with him."

"Someone needed to. Besides, I'm pretty sure Julian also talked to him. I'm serious, though. You could open the door and stay in your bedroom while he sits here in the hallway. I'll tell everyone else to stay away, and you'll be able to talk. You can see him, but as long as you keep the lights off in your bedroom, he won't be able to see you. You'll have all the power in your hands."

"It's not fair to him. I shouldn't have all the power."

"Life isn't fair. You have to deal with whatever it hands you, and this is it. It's either that, or you don't see or talk to him. Do you really want to do it that way?"

Tony didn't. He knew it wasn't right to lead Sam on, but he supposed Sam already knew how bad the situation was. He would understand, at least for now.

And if in the future he decided this was too much and that he couldn't deal with it, well, Tony would have to accept that. He would even understand. He didn't want to lose Sam before he had a chance to be with him, but their situation was less than ideal. Like Miles had said, they had to do the most with what they had, and maybe this was the first step to make that happen.

Sam kept peeking at the stairs. He knew there was no way Tony was coming downstairs to talk to him, but no matter how many times he told himself that, he couldn't seem to stop.

Julian was right. If Sam was planning on being in Tony's

life, he needed to get used to being around the council assassins. They were normal people, just like he'd expected. He'd understood a long time ago that their job didn't make them different or bad. It seemed like he hadn't made it known, though, and he disliked the thought that his brother thought Sam believed him to be a monster.

Julian wasn't a monster. He was strange and annoying, but not a monster.

"He's not going to come," Julian said loud enough that a few people around the table turned around.

Sam avoided looking at them. They were all nice people, but he didn't want to see the pity in their eyes. Julian might be annoying, but there was no pity in him. He understood the situation, and he believed it wasn't as desperate as Sam thought it might be. Sam didn't have his faith, but maybe he should. After all, Julian knew Tony better than Sam.

"I know. I didn't expect him to," Sam told him before spearing a piece of carrot on his plate and eating it.

"So you're not here to talk to him?"

"I'm here because you insisted I had to spend time with these people."

"Well, you do. They're Tony's family, so you might as well start now."

"Shouldn't I get to know Tony first?"

"Probably, but that's not going to be as easy as talking to his family."

Sam thought back to the texts he'd sent Tony that day. It was only the first step in what he hoped would be a normal relationship, although he wasn't quite sure what normal would entail. What he did know was that he was telling Tony about himself, and that hopefully, it meant Tony would start to trust him in time. Once that happened, Sam could get to know Tony, too.

It wasn't going to happen anytime soon, but it was yet

another step toward that goal, and it made him feel better about coming tonight.

He'd already met all the assassins, so he'd known what to expect. Just like the last time he'd been here, they acted like a big family. There was nothing strange here, nothing that betrayed the kind of work they did. It wasn't even like the house Sam had grown up in. There were no guns around, no talking about work over the dinner table. Everyone was relaxed and talking and laughing, and it made him feel like he belonged, even though he definitely didn't.

He wasn't the only non-assassin at the table, though. He'd been introduced to all the mates who were present, which included a lawyer, the cook, a computer nerd, and a scientist. Sam wasn't sure he belonged in that group, either, but he supposed that, in a way, he did. He was a council assassin's mate just like them, no matter how different he was from them.

A movement on the stairs made him turn around again. It wasn't Tony, but Miles, who had been upstairs to talk to Tony. Sam held his breath, wondering what had happened and if it would have anything to do with him. He almost smiled when Miles made a beeline for him, even though he had no idea what Miles wanted to tell him yet.

"Hi," Miles said when he reached Sam.

Sam smiled at him. "We already said hi when I arrived."

Miles grinned and shrugged. "Still. It's not like we talked since then." He leaned closer. "I talked to Tony."

"How is he?" Sam desperately needed to know what they'd talked about, but he didn't want to be nosy.

"Still the same. He agreed to talk to you, though."

Suddenly, Sam couldn't breathe. "He did?" he asked, reaching for his glass of water.

"I have to explain to you how he wants to do this first."

"I'm listening." Sam was ready to do pretty much anything for the chance to talk to his mate.

Miles crouched next to Sam's chair so he wouldn't be standing over him. "He's going to open his bedroom door so you don't have to talk through the door. I'm not sure if he's going to allow you to see him, but he'll be able to see you. He wants you to stay in the hallway while he'll be in his bedroom. I guess you can sit in front of the door or something. I know it's not ideal, but it was already hard enough to convince him to open the door. I don't think I can help any more than I already have."

"It's fine. I can imagine how hard it is, and I don't expect anything from him. If it's more comfortable, we can talk through the door."

Miles smiled. "It's great you feel that way, but it's good that he agreed to open the door. He needs to start dealing with how he feels and what happened to him, and he hasn't been. Trying to ignore it isn't going to help. Hopefully, having you in his life will push him in the right direction."

It was a lot to put on Sam's shoulders, and for anyone else, it would have terrified him. But Tony was his mate, and Sam was willing to do a lot to help him.

Sam followed Miles upstairs right away, not caring about dinner anymore. He'd been here the other day when he'd helped Julian move, but he didn't know which bedroom belonged to Tony. He was eager to get to know everything he could about his mate, and that included details like this one.

Miles stopped in front of a bedroom. The door was still closed, and he knocked. "Tony? Sam and I are here. How about Sam sits in front of the door, and you open it?"

There was movement inside the room, and when Tony answered, he sounded much closer than Sam had expected. "Are you going to stay around?"

"Only if you want me to."

"You can go back downstairs."

Sam's eyes went wide. He'd expected Tony to want Miles

51

to stay in case he needed protection. The fact that he trusted Sam enough to be alone with him with the door open touched him more than he'd expected.

"All right," Miles answered. "You know you only have to scream for someone to come upstairs." He looked at Sam. "Good luck," he murmured.

Then he was gone.

Sam didn't waste time. He sat on the floor facing Tony's bedroom door. He almost expected Tony not to open, and he couldn't help but smile when he heard the sound of the door unlocking. It gently pulled open, but Sam couldn't see anything, since the room behind it was dark. It was a bit disappointing, but this was already a lot for Tony, and Sam was grateful for any scrap he got.

There was the sound of footsteps, then a light clicked on on the nightstand, illuminating Tony, who was sitting on the bed. His back was ramrod straight, which was enough for Sam to know how hard it was for him.

Sam smiled and waved. "Hi. It's great to see you again."

Tony chuckled nervously. "I can't say I actually saw you the first time we met."

"You were overwhelmed. I shouldn't have come up to you the way I did."

"Why not? You could have done it without a problem with anyone else. It's not fair to ask you to behave differently just because of what happened to me."

Sam frowned. He'd already known it would take time for Tony to trust him and start healing, so he wasn't surprised at the words. He still didn't like Tony talking about himself that way. "I don't think we can talk about something being fair or not in this situation. We can't change what happened to you or how you're reacting to it. It's going to take time, and I don't mind it."

"It's not fair to you to be stuck with me, though."

"I don't see it as being stuck with you. As far as I'm concerned, being with your mate is always hard work. I can't imagine Tali has an easy time sticking with my brother."

Tony laughed. "Maybe that's why he didn't want to talk to him in the beginning."

Sam gasped. "You're going to have to tell me everything about that. Julian never mentioned it, and I can't wait to hold it over his head."

Tony was silent, which told Sam he was nervous. Sam wanted to help him however he could, and he had an idea. "Are you afraid of rabbits?"

He could see Tony blink from a distance. "Of course not. Who's afraid of rabbits?"

"I'm sure some people are. I asked because I was wondering if you'd be more comfortable if I shifted. I'm a rabbit shifter, like Julian. We're fairly harmless in that form."

"I doubt Julian is harmless in any form, but you're not him."

"I'm not. I'm not trained to do anything dangerous like he can. I can shift, and I can either stay here or come closer if you're comfortable with that."

"Can I stroke your fur?"

Sam hadn't expected that, but he was more than happy for Tony to do it. "Of course. I love being cuddled."

"I guess we can try."

Sam almost couldn't believe it, but he wasn't going to back down. He quickly made sure he wouldn't end up tangled in his clothes, then he shifted. He didn't have to strip naked in front of Tony, thankfully. That would probably make Tony even more uncomfortable than he already was. But he was small enough to be able to wiggle his way out of his clothes once he'd shifted, and when he did, he carefully hopped toward the door.

Tony was still on the bed, staring at Sam. Sam stayed where

he was, knowing better than to intrude in Tony's private space.

Tony climbed off the bed and came closer. He didn't leave the bedroom, but he sat next to the door and reached out. His fingers trembled when he touched the top of Sam's head, and Sam made sure not to move and startle him. After a moment, Tony's movements became firmer, and Sam hoped it meant he was relaxing.

"So, you've texted me about yourself the entire day, and I didn't answer. I'm sorry. I should have, but it was hard to push myself to do it. I guess we can turn things around now, since I can speak, but you can't answer."

Tony pressed his back against the wall by the door and looked up at the ceiling. He was still stroking Sam, and Sam settled in to listen. This was a lot more than he'd expected would happen, and he was happy about it. It wasn't just one step forward. It was several of them, and hopefully, it would show Tony that he could trust him, even if it was only in his rabbit form. He was ready to spend most of his time like this if it meant Tony was comfortable with his presence for as long as Tony needed him to.

CHAPTER FOUR

Tony stared at his reflection in the mirror. He didn't look any different than he had a week or a month ago, but he *felt* different. He wasn't sure what it meant for him, but it had a lot to do with Sam, if not everything.

Their conversation had been strange and stilted, but it had been a conversation, which was more than Tony had expected and hoped would happen. He knew he should be grateful that Sam wasn't already pushing for more. As it was, he'd continued texting Tony, apparently not expecting an answer. That was good, because most days, Tony didn't think he was capable of answering. The thought of doing it scared him, and he wasn't even sure why.

He didn't want to give Sam false hope, he supposed. If he answered, Sam might think he was healed or something, which wasn't the case. But maybe he should give Sam more credit. He was aware of what was happening, and he didn't expect more than Tony was ready to give.

What did that mean for them? They were mates, but Tony couldn't act like a mate. No matter how much he wanted to, the thought of Sam touching him sent him into a panic, with his werewolf grumbling in the back of his mind. The damn thing probably felt Tony was weak, and Tony wouldn't disagree.

He wanted to be better, both for Sam and for himself. After everything he'd gone through, he deserved to be happy. He shouldn't be hiding in his bedroom day in and day out, staying away from the people who loved him and from what he and Sam could have together. It wasn't fair, and he felt that he should let Sam go if he wasn't going to try to change things. He was pretty sure that if he tried telling Sam that, though, Sam would try kicking his ass at a distance. He was as stubborn as Tony, which didn't bode well for their future relationship—if they ever managed to have one.

Tony would never find out if he didn't change something. He already knew what his first step was supposed to be, and while he wasn't looking forward to it, he thought he was ready to take it. Some people might think that doing it for Sam wasn't a good reason and that Tony should be doing it for himself, but right now, Tony didn't think he could do anything for himself. He wanted to give Sam what he deserved, though, and for now, he hadn't been able to.

He pushed away from the bathroom sink and went back to his bedroom. The room was quiet, just like always, and it made Tony's chest squeeze painfully. He could hear the others somewhere in the house, talking and laughing, and he wanted to be part of that again. His friends would welcome him if he went downstairs, but he would freak out, which was the last thing he needed. He had to do this, whatever *this* was, slowly and carefully.

That was why instead of heading downstairs, he moved toward the dresser. He'd left his phone there, and he smiled when he saw there was another text from Sam, lamenting the fact that his newest clients were impossible to please.

Instead of answering or staring at his phone for an hour hoping Sam would text again, Tony opened his list of contacts and looked for the one he was searching for.

He wasn't an idiot. He understood what was happening to him, and he knew what to do to start healing from it. He'd already gone through it once. He was strong enough to do it a second time, or at least, he hoped so.

He found the number he was looking for and tapped on it

to call before changing his mind. His fingers were trembling and his hands felt sweaty, and he had to swallow several times as he waited for Gentry to answer.

"Hello?"

Gentry was a psychologist who lived in Gillham. He'd worked a lot with shifters and humans who had managed to escape from the labs in the past twenty years, and Tony had talked to him when he'd first become a council assassin. As far as he knew, Gentry had worked with all the assassins, trying to help them get over what had been done to them and to deal with what they still did to this day. Tony already knew him, and he was pretty sure Gentry had been told about what had happened to him recently. Tony's call wouldn't be a surprise.

"It's Tony. The council assassin," Tony murmured. His voice felt raw, more so than it should have been.

"I was expecting your call, although I'd been warned you wouldn't contact me."

Tony chuckled deprecatingly. "I probably wouldn't be calling you if I hadn't met my mate and if I didn't think he deserves more than I could give him right now."

Gentry didn't sound surprised. "That's new. Can I congratulate you, or is it complicated?"

"I'm not sure yet. I'm honestly torn between being happy at meeting Sam and knowing I'm not good enough for him and that I can't give him what he deserves."

"And that's why you called?"

"I know Win talked to you."

"He did. I would like for *you* to tell me what happened, though."

Of course he did. Tony didn't want to talk about it, but he'd called Gentry knowing that was how he worked. "I was taken on a mission recently. Captured. They tortured me to find the location of the warehouse, and I gave it to them."

"But you managed to escape," Gentry said when Tony didn't continue.

"I had to. I'd given away the location of the warehouse, and I had to warn everyone. I couldn't let them pay for what I'd done."

"What you'd done? I doubt you gave yourself up. The torture was something that was done to you, not something you did or caused."

Tony sighed. This was where things got complicated. "I know that." There was no way for him to control what those people had done. He'd tried his best, both to escape and to resist the torture, but in the end, he'd broken down, just like anyone would have. "I still feel guilty and weak. I shouldn't have said anything."

"And they probably would have killed you if you hadn't. I suspect they would have found another way to get to the warehouse, probably by torturing one of your friends."

The thought made Tony want to cry. "I know all of that, rationally. I know it wasn't my fault and that anyone would have broken. I also know I should get over it. It's what Sam deserves."

Gentry was silent for a moment. "It's obvious that it's going to take more than a phone conversation for you to start healing from this. Do you think we can work together? We can continue having conversations anytime you need them, but I'd like to set up a schedule."

"Please. That's why I called. I know I need help, and I'm finally ready to accept it."

"For Sam?"

Tony knew Gentry wouldn't judge him if he said yes. "For Sam, but also for myself. I don't want to do this anymore. I survived. I should live, since I have the opportunity to do it, but I can't right now. It's not fair to Sam or me."

"Good."

They spent the next ten minutes discussing how often Gentry wanted to talk to Tony and how they would make it work. Gentry had to shift things around his schedule, but they managed to find a way to make it work for both of them, and by the time they hung up, Tony felt better.

He was nowhere near close to being healed, but he'd taken the first step toward that, and he felt good. He felt so good that he stuck his phone in his pocket and threw open his bedroom door.

The hallway was empty. He could hear voices downstairs and the sound of pots and pans banging together. Something was cooking, and he realized it was almost lunchtime. He couldn't remember the last time he'd had lunch with his family, but he knew it had been before he was captured. He wasn't sure he could actually sit down with them today, but for the first time since he'd come back, Tony felt like he should try. It didn't matter how he felt about it, how terrified he was. He knew his family wouldn't hurt him, and he kept that in mind as he slowly walked down the stairs. Even if he decided to run back to his bedroom, no one would care. Whoever was home would be happy to see him, and he would be happy to see them, even though he was also terrified.

He could do this. Calling Gentry had been the first step, and now, Tony needed to take more of them.

Sam realized he was humming as he worked, something he never did. He knew what had caused it, but it didn't make sense. He and Tony only had one conversation. Tony still wasn't answering most of Sam's texts, and while that wasn't going to make him stop sending them, it also made him wonder just how hard this would be. Apparently, it didn't matter. He was happy, and while he didn't understand why considering how hard all of this would be, he decided to go along with it.

Of course he was happy. He'd met his mate, and the complications didn't matter. Things would get harder sooner rather than later, but in the meantime, he wanted to enjoy the feeling of having Tony in his life and the possibility of a relationship with him.

Then he remembered he had a family dinner tonight, and he stopped humming.

He loved his family, but they were too different. Sam had never gotten along with them, and he realized it was his fault. He'd kept himself separated because he wanted them to know he was different, and now, he never quite knew how to behave with them. He still went to family dinners, bought them birthday and Christmas presents, and he did his best to be family to them, but he also avoided them any time he could. Now, he wondered why he'd done that to begin with.

He didn't like the kind of job his parents and his siblings did, but he understood that sometimes it was necessary. Most people would have been horrified at the thought, but Sam wasn't. His family might be made up of professional killers, but they didn't just kill anyone they wanted or were hired to kill. They'd always had a code they followed, and that hadn't changed.

It was a similar to the code the council assassins followed, or rather, the one the council followed. Julian had told Sam that council only had people killed that they couldn't deal with in any other way. He'd mentioned people who trafficked children and other shifters as pets, and Sam could imagine that was only the tip of the iceberg. He might never understand how someone could become a professional killer, but he did understand the need for them, and he wasn't going to berate them for the work they did.

He would have to become more comfortable with being around people who killed for a living if he wanted any kind of relationship with Tony. He wasn't sure how things would go between them, but he wasn't going to give up until Tony asked him to, which meant that even though he'd tried to avoid it all his life, he would have to deal with the reality of professional assassins.

That didn't mean he had to start enjoying having dinner with his family suddenly.

His problem with them wasn't just the professional killers thing. It was also the fact that Julian was mouthy and couldn't keep secrets to save his life, while Kara tended to be too protective when it came to Sam. She often offered to kill his exes, something he'd been tempted to accept a few times. Thankfully, he hadn't allowed the grief over past relationships to influence him. If it was up to his sister, he would leave a trail of dead exes in his path.

"Hello?" someone called out from the door.

Sam shook himself, pasted a smile on his face, and turned to welcome the first visitor of this open house. "Good morning," he said.

The rest of the day was a blur. Sam was used to openhouses and all the work that went into them, but that didn't make it easier. By the time he finally locked the door behind himself, he was exhausted and unsure if he was up to having dinner with his parents and siblings. They would hunt him down if he didn't go, so instead of heading toward his house, he drove toward the house where he grew up.

He parked in the driveway, turned off the engine, and took a moment to breathe. Hopefully, Julian hadn't told the rest of the family about Tony yet. They were going to be over the moon happy for Sam, and they could be a bit much most of the time. Considering what Tony was going through, they would have to be careful. Sam was protective of his mate, and that included protecting him from his overbearing parents and overexcited siblings.

The driver's door opened, and Julian stood there, staring down at Sam. "What's going on? Are you dying?"

Sam rolled his eyes and pushed his brother away so he could get out of the car. "I wish. If I died, I wouldn't have to have dinner with you."

Julian pressed a hand against his chest. "I'm wounded."

"Wouldn't you be talking less if you were wounded? No, wait. Of course you wouldn't. You're *you*. You're going to talk until you drop dead."

Julian grinned and knocked his shoulder against Sam's. "I know you love me, even though you try hard to hide it."

"The fact that you think I'm hiding my love for you is worrying. Did you get hit on the head recently?"

"Well, my mate tried to knock me out, but I think that was because I wouldn't let him sleep and I kept talking."

"That would do the trick." Sam wasn't sure what he would have done if his mate had been like his brother. Tali was braver than anyone Sam knew.

He followed Julian up the driveway toward the house. Julian was still talking, but then, he always did. That was why it took Sam a moment to realize what he was talking about, or rather, who. "Can you repeat that?" he asked as they reached the front door.

Julian didn't look offended. He was probably used to Sam not listening to him when he talked. "Tony came downstairs for lunch today."

Sam's mouth was dry. "On his own?"

"What, you think we would force him?"

"No. It's just that I didn't expect it."

"No one did. We were all surprised, and while it was obvious he was ready to bolt at any second, he stayed until the end of the meal. He even ate, and even though he disappeared as soon as he was done, it's progress. I don't know what happened, but I was happy to see him there."

Sam resisted the urge to check his phone. He wanted to text Tony and make sure he was okay, but he also didn't want Tony to think he believed he was weak or anything like that. Sam was aware that it was a big problem for Tony. He didn't want to be vulnerable, and he thought he was broken. There was nothing further from the truth, but no matter how many times Sam told him that, he doubted Tony would believe him. Tony had to show himself he wasn't broken, and maybe, he was finally starting to do it.

"Who are you two talking about?" Sam's mother asked as she came closer to kiss Sam on the cheek.

Sam tried to tell his brother not to say anything with his eyes, but Julian gleefully ignored him and turned to their mother. "Sam's mate."

Their mom sucked in a breath and turned to Sam. "You found your mate?"

Sam sighed. He should have known something like this would happen, and he supposed he was going to spend the rest of the evening explaining why his family couldn't meet Tony just yet.

It took a while for them to hear the entire story and to understand, and by the end of it, Sam was even more tired. He disappeared into the bathroom to take a break, even though it would be a short one, and he took advantage of that time alone to text Tony. He didn't expect an answer, which was why he almost dropped the phone into the toilet when it vibrated in his hand.

Thanks for checking in. I'm fine, and I'm surprised I am.

Sam smiled at the phone. *That's great.*

It took Tony a moment to answer that text. Sam would have thought he wasn't going to if he hadn't seen the three dots waving on his screen.

Do you want to come over?

Sam blinked at the screen. *You mean tonight?*

Yes, please. We can do the same thing we did the last time you were here.

Sam shuddered at the thought. They hadn't done much, but he was looking forward to a similar evening. It had felt good to be cuddled by Tony and to listen to him talk about himself. *I'll be there as soon as I can.*

Tony couldn't ask Sam not to come when he'd told him to come only a few minutes ago, right?

He stared at his phone, wondering if he'd made a mistake. He wanted to see Sam and to talk to him, but he was also terrified.

He swallowed and tried to think logically instead of letting his fear and feelings take over. He'd already asked Sam to come over, and he wouldn't go back on that. Besides, he knew Sam well enough by now to be sure his mate would stay away or back off if Tony needed him to. Tony disliked that Sam and everyone else had to treat him like he was fragile, but he knew he was. They weren't wrong to treat him that way.

So he and Sam would do what they'd done the last time. Tony had enjoyed talking to Sam and telling him about his life before he was tortured the second time, and he'd enjoyed stroking Sam's soft fur just as much. It was easier to talk to him when he was in his rabbit form, and Tony hoped Sam wasn't offended by that.

Still, Tony needed to talk to someone right now, before he freaked out, and who better than Miles?

Tony only realized what he was doing once he was already in the hallway outside his bedroom and headed toward Miles's. He'd left his bedroom without even thinking about it twice. Going downstairs for lunch today had been hard, but this time, he hadn't even hesitated.

He stopped in the middle of the hallway and swallowed. He was nowhere near healed, but he truly felt like he'd finally turned the page and like he was taking his life into his own hands and moving forward instead of staying still and allowing the people who had tortured him to ruin the rest of his life.

He was alive. He'd made it out, and no matter how hard it was, he was going to enjoy the rest of his life.

He knocked on Miles's door. His palms were sweaty, and he rubbed them onto his thighs. Miles opened the door, smiling, and his eyes went wide when he saw Tony standing there. "Holy shit. What happened to you today?" he asked.

Tony pushed past him and stepped into the bedroom. He felt calmer once he was there and the door was closed. He trusted everyone in the house, but he didn't like feeling exposed, not even to them. He was safe in Miles's bedroom, though. He took a deep breath, then faced his best friend. "I asked Sam to come over," he said instead of answering Miles's question. He wouldn't have been sure how to answer it anyway.

Miles slowly nodded. "That's good, right?"

"It is, but I'm freaking out. I don't think I can stop."

Miles came closer but still kept his distance. "What did you tell him?"

"I asked him if he wanted to come over, and I said we could do what we did the last time he was here."

"Which is cuddle him in his rabbit form, right?"

Tony hoped he wasn't blushing. "It is. I talked a lot, more than I expected, and he seemed to enjoy it. Or maybe he was enjoying me cuddling him. I'm not sure."

Miles chuckled. "I'm pretty sure he enjoyed both. Is he okay with doing it again?"

"He seems to be. He said yes."

"Good. Do you want me to set things up like I did the last time? You can sit on your bed, and I'll come upstairs with Sam once he arrives. I'll open the door, and you won't have to go anywhere near him until he shifts."

Tony nodded, but he had something else on his mind. "I know that doing this isn't fair to Sam."

Miles crossed his arms over his chest. "Did he tell you that?"

"He wouldn't. But I'm not an idiot. We're mates, and we should do more than cuddling, especially since he stayed in his rabbit form the entire time."

"Maybe, maybe not. You might be mates, but it doesn't mean you have to do anything. There are no rules. You can take it as fast or as slow as you want. I'm sure Sam agrees, and it might be a good idea to talk to him about it. Maybe mention it while you're petting him?"

Tony glared at Miles, even though he didn't have a good reason to. Miles wasn't making fun or teasing him. He was genuinely trying to find a way for Tony to feel more comfortable with Sam, and Tony was grateful.

"I'll talk to him," he promised.

Miles beamed. "Good. Why don't you grab a shower? I'll go downstairs and wait for Sam to arrive. I can bring him up as soon as he's here, and I'll take care of everything else, too. You just have to relax."

Tony wasn't sure that was possible, but he was going to try.

He headed back to his bedroom. His heart was racing, and things would only get worse once Sam was here. Tony wanted to do this, though, and for the first time, he felt as if he and Sam truly could make things work. He had no idea what the future would look like for them, but he wasn't ready to give up — on himself or on his relationship with Sam.

Because Sam wasn't just a guy. He was Tony's mate, and he wouldn't be if Tony couldn't trust him. Tony was aware that not all mates made things work in the end, but those who didn't were an oddity, and Tony had no intention of being part of that group.

His life was already odd enough as it was without adding that to it.

Once in the shower, he let the warm water relax him, but it wasn't easy. He couldn't help but think that he probably wouldn't have met Sam if he hadn't been captured and tortured. He didn't like to think about it, but he couldn't deny it. Some people thought that mates met when they needed it the most, and maybe that was what had happened here. Tony needed Sam in his life to show him there was more to him than what had been done in the labs or when he'd been tortured. He needed to show Tony he could live without being afraid, that he deserved more than the small life he had now, and that he could leave the pain and fear behind.

It was a lot to put on someone's shoulders, but Tony was pretty sure Sam would be up for the job. He didn't look like a quitter, something for which Tony was relieved. A lot of men would have run the other way after understanding what Tony had been through and how complicated the relationship would be, but Sam hadn't. He was still here, supporting Tony and allowing him to take things at his own pace. He wouldn't push for anything Tony wasn't ready to give, which made him perfect for Tony.

Maybe there *was* some truth in the theory that mates only met when they needed to meet.

Tony walked out of the shower feeling better but still nervous. He was afraid that Sam would eventually realize he was too much work or that he would take advantage of Tony's vulnerability in some way, but Tony told himself he had to forget about that. Those were his fears talking, the part of his mind that still thought he was broken. It was a part of him that didn't believe he deserved what Sam could offer him. It was something he had to get over, and while it wasn't going to be easy by any means, he felt he was moving in the right direction.

A knock on the door made him jump. "Tony? Sam is here," Miles said.

Tony sucked in a breath. He looked at himself in the mirror one last time, hoping Sam would like what he'd see. After the shower, Tony had dressed in soft pajama pants and a t-shirt. He hadn't bothered styling his hair, and it was still damp and falling over his forehead. He needed a haircut, but he couldn't trust anyone to come that close to him, especially with a sharp object in hand.

He wasn't going to be any more ready than he already was, so he turned toward the bedroom door. "You can open," he said, praying everything would go the way it was supposed to go — the way he hoped things would go.

Sam was nervous. He'd expected something like this to happen, so he hadn't been surprised to find Miles waiting for him when he arrived. He was still stunned that the assassins hadn't hesitated to give him the code that would open the doors downstairs and let him in through the security system. They trusted him, which didn't make sense to him, but he wasn't going to protest, not when it gave him easy access to Tony.

Miles had quickly explained that while Tony was eager to see Sam, he was also still wary, and he wanted to do things the way they had the last time Sam was here. That was more than okay with Sam. He'd enjoyed listening to Tony and being cuddled, and he was looking forward to doing it again.

He realized that Tony found him less intimidating when he was in his rabbit form, and he was ready to shift any time Tony needed him to. He hadn't imagined things between him and his mate would go that way, but it was better than nothing, and if it kept Tony comfortable and happy, the same went for Sam.

Miles turned to smile at Sam as he opened the door to Tony's bedroom. "I'm going to go back downstairs," he explained.

Sam wasn't looking at him anymore. He peered inside the bedroom, smiling when he saw Tony sitting on his bed. He looked like he'd just showered, and the sight made Sam's mouth go dry.

They were nowhere near close to being intimate the way Sam hoped they would be eventually. He had a healthy sex drive, which meant that yes, he wanted to get Tony into bed and have his way with him. He wasn't stupid, though. He wouldn't do anything to ruin what he and Tony were building, and if it meant having to wait years to have sex again, he would do it. He wasn't ruled by his dick, even though some days, it felt like it.

"And I just lost both of you," Miles drawled.

Sam forced himself to turn his attention back to him. "I'm sorry."

Miles shook his head. "Don't be. I'm happy for you and Tony, and I'm out of here. Have fun. You know where the door is when you want to leave."

With that, he turned around and walked down the hallway.

Sam looked back at Tony. "Do you want me to shift right away?"

Tony shook his head. "We can talk a bit first. I know that having only one of us talk isn't the greatest way to get to know each other."

Sam nodded and sat on the floor just outside the door. He wasn't on the other side of the hallway like they'd started last time, and he hoped Tony wasn't uncomfortable. Hopefully, Tony would tell him if he was. "You're not wrong. Did you want to ask me anything?"

Tony hesitated. "Actually, yes. Julian has been coming

around. He stays outside of the door, just like you. He's been telling me about you."

Sam groaned. "Great. What exactly has he been saying?"

Tony chuckled. It sounded rusty but warm. "Nothing bad. But he mentioned that your entire family is made up of professional assassins except for you, and that it makes you uncomfortable. It made me think, since that's what I did before I was captured."

Sam had expected this to become a problem between them. He wouldn't let it, not if he could avoid it. It was something they needed to talk about, but it would only be a problem if he allowed it to turn into one. The best way not to make that happen was to talk about it, something he was ready to do. "I understand the need for professional assassins. I've heard enough from Julian and my sister, and even my parents, to know that some people can't be dealt with in any other way. They are too powerful and rich, and they manage to sneak their way out of the system. And of course, you and your friends work for the council."

"That doesn't mean we do the right thing," Tony pointed out. "We follow orders, and we're not the ones who decide who dies."

"I'm sure the council makes mistakes, but they can't order you to kill someone unilaterally, right? They make those decisions as a group, which in my opinion, helps make sure it's the right ones."

"So you don't hate the profession as a whole?"

"I never did. But I won't deny that I grew up resentful. My father was the only one who did the job when I was a kid and a teenager, and it brought in a lot of money. Both Julian and my sister were happy about it, but I disliked not being able to tell my friends what my father did or to bring them home. None of my family members have ever been shy when it comes to talking about the job. They don't hide it, which means there would often be guns on the dinner table, and the conversations over family meals were more often than not uncomfortable. That resentment is the main reason I decided not to follow in my father's footsteps. Both Julian and our sister did, but I went for a profession that was as different from that as I could find."

"You sell houses."

Sam nodded. "I see Julian told you about that, too."

"I doubt there's much Julian hasn't told me. He seems pretty excited at the thought that we're mates."

"I think he wants both of us to be happy. He's . . . strange, but he cares."

"I'm not working right now, and I don't know if I'll ever be able to go back on the job, but do you think this will become a problem between us if I do?"

Sam had thought about it. He'd barely been able to think about anything that wasn't Tony since they'd met. He'd known that this could become a problem if he let it, and he wasn't willing to do that, not with all the other problems they already had. "It won't. As long as *I* don't have to do that kind of work, I can deal with it."

Tony nodded. "Do you like your job, then?"

Sam sighed. "I tell everyone I do."

"That's not the same as actually liking it."

"I like taking care of people, and in a way, finding them a forever home makes me happy. I hate having to deal with difficult clients, though. I hate how I don't have set hours and how exhausted I am by the end of the day. It's also hard to build yourself a life when you know that you're one failed sale away from being broke."

"Why not find another job if you don't like it?"

Sam shrugged. "It's not as easy as it sounds. I would love to get another job, but I'm not willing to give this one up, not when I'm not sure I can find something else. My family would help me if I asked them, but I can't."

"You're too proud."

"Maybe it's pride, or maybe I just want to stand on my own two feet."

"What would you do if you could choose?"

"I don't know. I just want to take care of people and make them happy, so maybe something along those lines? I'd like to simplify people's lives, if that makes sense."

"I think it does. I also think you'd be perfect at it."

Sam wasn't too sure about that. "I don't know about you, but I'm done talking about my job. Is it time to cuddle yet?"

Tony laughed. "You enjoy it, don't you?"

"Very much so, and I don't often have the opportunity to have a gorgeous man stroke my fur."

Tony arched a brow. "I would have thought the opposite."

"Didn't you hear me mention the fact that I'm over-worked? I don't have time for a social life, and it's not the same to have Julian or Kara do it."

"Why don't you come here and shift, then?"

That was a huge concession for Tony. He was inviting Sam into his personal space, the only space he felt safe.

Sam didn't ask him if he was sure. Tony wouldn't have of-fered if he wasn't, so Sam got to his feet, stepped into the bed-room, and closed the door behind himself. Then, before Tony could start getting nervous, Sam shifted and wriggled out of his clothes. He hopped closer to the bed, hoping Tony wasn't freaking out.

Tony appeared at the edge of the mattress. He reached for Sam, and Sam allowed him to catch him and hold him close. Instead of putting Sam onto the bed, Tony held him against his chest and buried his face into Sam's fur. A sob escaped him, but Sam didn't think he was crying.

This was so much more than he'd expected to happen, and he was happy. It would take time, but he could see him and

Tony working things out and being happy together, no matter what had happened in the past or what happened in the future.

Sam would wait for Tony forever if he had to.

CHAPTER FIVE

Tony often wondered if things would ever go back to normal, or at least, to the normal he was used to. He wanted to believe it would, but things were slow going, even though he was now working with Gentry. Going back to a normal life felt out of reach, and no matter how many times he'd told himself that he just needed time, he couldn't help but wonder if that was the case.

He still felt broken. No one else thought he was, but he couldn't hide the truth, not from himself. He might be working on getting back to what he'd been before, but he doubted it would happen, not anytime soon. He felt vulnerable. It made him want to hide, but lately, he'd been forcing himself to spend more time with his friends, and he was finally more comfortable with it.

Even though he was broken, he wanted to give himself a chance, and more importantly, he wanted to give himself and Sam a chance. That wouldn't happen if he kept on hiding and if he focused on the bad things. Sam deserved better, and so did Tony.

Tony suspected a lot of people would tell him that Sam wasn't a good reason to heal. Tony should be doing this for himself because he wanted to get better, and he did. He also knew that if Sam hadn't stepped into his life, he wouldn't have done this. If he wasn't going to lie to himself about being broken, he also couldn't lie to himself about this. He was stubborn, and if he hadn't had Sam, he would still be hiding in his bedroom, pushing everyone away. He wanted to be happy, and he wanted to be with Sam. For now, those two reasons were more than enough for him to finally make changes, and that was all that mattered.

He looked around the living room. It was noisy, but then it always was. With so many people living in the warehouse, there was always someone home, and they tended to gather in the living room and kitchen, which was one big area. Tony had always loved that, and he still did, even though it made him nervous. No one here would hurt him, which he had to keep in mind. They wanted Tony to heal as much as Tony wanted to, and he suspected that if they had their way, they would already have killed the people who had tortured him in the hope it would help him.

He tightened his hands into fists so hard that his nails dug into his palms. He was still afraid of those people, but now that he was finally allowing himself to heal, he was also angry. They'd ruined his life, not once, but twice. They might not have been the same people who had captured him the first time and had turned him into what he was now, but that didn't mean his life wasn't ruined. He had to start from step one again, and he hadn't been ready for that. He doubted anyone would be, not after what he'd already lived through.

The people who had tortured him had taken so much from him. They'd taken the place he'd called home for years, the only safe place he and the others had. They'd moved, and they were safe now, too, but this warehouse didn't feel like home yet. It looked a lot like the old one, but it didn't hold the same memories, and it made Tony twitchy.

But then, a lot of things did these days.

A hand landed on his shoulder, and he reacted before he could think. Logically, he knew that whoever was touching him didn't mean him any harm. It was no doubt one of his friends, since the only people who could come into the warehouse were them and their mates. Not even council members were allowed in.

None of that mattered to Tony. When the hand squeezed his shoulder from behind, he jumped off the couch, twirling around and shifting as he did so. His clothes exploded around him, the shreds drifting to the floor as he faced his attacker. His breathing was harsh, and it didn't help when he found himself face to face with a rounded-eyed Armand.

Armand raised his hands as he stumbled back. He was trying to make himself look harmless, even though he was anything but. "Sorry. I didn't mean to scare you. I should have thought better about what I was doing."

He should have, but then he often didn't think much. Anyone else would have known that coming from behind and touching Tony without telling him they were there would lead to a disaster. Armand was lucky Tony hadn't lashed out and had limited himself to shifting.

Tony swallowed, horror gripping his stomach. He could have seriously hurt Armand, and he never wanted something like that to happen. He didn't want to hurt his friends, his family, or his mate. He didn't want to be a danger to any of them.

But he was, and maybe it would be better for him to go back to his bedroom and stay there.

"Don't do that," Armand snapped.

Tony blinked at him.

Armand gestured at Tony's face. "You're freaking out and thinking you should go back to hiding. That's bullshit, and I hope you realize that once you can think clearly." He paused and rubbed his hands together. "Also, if you could dial down the cold, I'd be grateful."

Tony hadn't even realized he was using his power. He dialed it down instantly.

Armand smiled. "Better. Again, I'm sorry I startled you. I wasn't thinking."

"Do you *ever* think?" Miles asked from the kitchen island. He was sitting there playing on his phone, and while there was a teasing accent in his voice, he was tense, and Tony knew he would intervene if Tony needed him to.

"Why does everyone ask that?" Armand whined. "I think. Maybe not as much as I should, but I'm not a complete idiot."

"No one said you were," Beck, Armand's mate, said. He didn't even look up from his computer. "But sometimes, you *act* like you are, and that's not a good thing."

"Don't you love me anymore?" Armand cried out.

Tony found himself relaxing without conscious thought. He shifted back to his human form, snatching one of the blankets on the couch and wrapping it around himself.

"Eww, naked Tony butt on the blanket," Armand said. "Remind me not to use that one."

Tony's knees felt weak, and he sat down on the edge of the couch. Armand had reacted in the best way possible. Instead of making things worse, he'd lightened the mood, and Tony had been able to relax and realize that Armand didn't mean any harm. Whatever the reason he'd touched Tony, he truly hadn't meant to scare him. Tony was safe, and he had to remember that.

He had a long way to go, and he couldn't wait to get to the end of this. He was tired of being afraid, even of people he knew would never hurt him. He was tired of hiding, of not being able to go on missions. He wanted to go back to work, but he couldn't, not when even a friendly touch made him slip up.

But he couldn't help the fact that he was afraid. Maybe if the people who'd hurt him were dead, he wouldn't be so frightened anymore—or maybe he would be, since most of that was in his mind. Now that the idea had popped up, though, he found that he couldn't stop thinking about it.

What if he could rid the world of the people who had

tortured him? It would be a favor to everyone. Tony wanted to heal, and eventually, he wanted to get back to work. He wouldn't be able to if he didn't first take care of this. Those people had hurt him, and they still were. The fear wouldn't stop until he made them disappear. Even if it didn't, he needed to do this.

But how could he when he could barely leave the warehouse? Could he really go on this mission? Could he find the people who had tortured him and kill them? And if he did, would it free him from his fear, or would he still be stuck in this house, afraid of the people who cared most about him?

He didn't have answers to those questions, but he wanted to find out. Even if he only managed to get out of the warehouse for this, it would still be a victory, and he needed one.

Sam still thought it was weird that he was always welcome at the warehouse, but he'd stopped wondering why. He suspected a lot of that had to do with his brother and with the fact that he was Tony's mate, and of course, with the background check the assassins had no doubt done on him. He had nothing to hide, and whoever had done the search had probably been bored to tears.

Sam didn't care that someone had dug into his past when the result was that he could come and go as he pleased and visit Tony whenever he wanted to. That was why he'd come today initially, but instead of being with Tony, he was spending time with Julian. They were in the gym, although Julian was the only one who was actually exercising. Sam was tired just looking at him, and he had no intention of even raising one finger.

He wasn't sure where he and Tony stood, which was why he'd looked for Julian instead of his mate. He and Tony were more comfortable with each other, but Sam was usually in his rabbit form when they spent time together. It made conversation tricky, and he hoped that eventually, they would get over this hurdle, but he wasn't going to push. They were doing this at Tony's pace, and that was that.

Besides, Sam had other things to think about. Even though he was welcome here and no one had tried to scare him, sometimes, he couldn't stop thinking about the fact that almost everyone in the warehouse had killed people and that they continue doing so for money.

But the council assassins were different from Sam's father and sister. They worked for the council, which made what they did a bit easier to understand. They rid the world of evil people who couldn't be dealt with in any other way, or at least, that was what Sam kept telling himself when he thought about it.

It wasn't always easy. It especially wasn't easy when his own brother was now a council assassin. Julian looked at home here in the warehouse with everyone else, while Sam was just a visitor. Would things be different if he and Tony were closer? Sam didn't know, and wondering was no use, not when they couldn't change what they were going through.

He'd made sure Miles told Tony he was in the house before they actually saw each other, just in case. He always texted Tony, too, but he felt like this was a better way to do it. This way, Tony could come and find him if he wanted to.

Lately, Tony had started coming out of his room more often, which was a pleasure to see. Sam suspected that Tony was more comfortable with him when they were surrounded by people, at least when Sam was in his human form. It was perfectly fine with Sam, and one of the reasons he did this. He would never tell anyone, but the other reason was that he enjoyed spending time with his brother and the other people who lived here.

Julian would tease him endlessly if he admitted that, which was the main reason Sam didn't. Now that he and Julian were spending more time together, though, Sam was starting to realize what a good person Julian was. What he did for a living didn't have anything to do with the person he was.

"Are you thinking about killing those people who hurt your mate?" Julian asked. He sat up on the bench where he'd been doing something with dumbbells. Those things looked heavy enough to kill a guy.

"Why does your mind go straight to killing people all the time?" Sam asked instead of answering. He'd never thought about killing people, not realistically.

Julian shrugged. "Because it's my job, and because I want to protect Tony."

"He's protected here."

"Nothing can happen to him while he's here, but that doesn't mean I don't want to get my hands on the people who hurt him. You should have seen him before. He was nothing like this, and I want that Tony back, even though I didn't know him anywhere as well as I do now."

"You can't just go around killing people because you don't like them."

Julian arched a brow. "It's not that I don't like them. The world would be a better place if they weren't in it."

Sam couldn't argue with that. "That doesn't mean we have to kill them."

"Why not? Those people captured Tony and tortured him. They're the reason he's in trouble right now. I also doubt he's the only person they did that to. I could go out there, find them, and kill them. Maybe it would help Tony."

"It's none of your business," Sam snapped. "It's Tony's decision, not yours. Besides, you shouldn't be the one doing it, even if Tony decides he wants it to happen."

"Who's going to do it? You?"

"Of course not. I'm not that kind of person."

Julian's expression shifted. "But I am, and so is your mate."

"I remember that every time I come here. I know what you and everyone else here does for a living."

"But you're not okay with it still. Do you think you'll ever be able to accept it? Because I'm pretty sure Tony wants to go back to work once he gets over what happened to him."

"If he does, I'll learn to deal with it. In the meantime, I don't see why I should think about killing people."

Julian sighed. "I want to help Tony, but I don't know how."

"You won't do it by going behind his back and killing people." But now that Julian had mentioned it, Sam wondered if maybe it would work.

Tony was afraid. That was the main reason he didn't leave the warehouse and the reason he and Sam still hadn't spent any time together while both of them were in human form. Sam wanted that to change, but he couldn't push Tony to do something he wasn't comfortable with. Would killing the people who had hurt him change that? Would it make it easier for him to relax and heal? Probably not, but there was a chance it might.

Sam realized that if it did, he would do it.

It wasn't like him, but then, he'd never had to deal with feelings for his mate before. Even though he and Tony were distant, they were spending time together, and Sam was falling in love with his mate. It would have been hard not to, not when Tony was, well, Tony. There was a reason he and Sam were mates, and Sam couldn't have found a man better suited to him. The fact that Tony was hurt and afraid made him want to hit something, and who better than the people who had done that to Tony?

Sam frowned. He wasn't a professional killer like his brother or Tony, but he also wasn't useless. He'd grown up in a family of professional assassins, after all. He'd watched both his siblings go into the business, and he had an idea how it worked. There was no way he could do something like that on his own or without talking to Tony, but he couldn't stop thinking about it now that Julian had mentioned it.

"You're considering it," Julian said. He sounded both surprised and proud.

Sam's first instinct was to deny it, but he would need help if he wanted to do this. "Maybe."

Julian beamed. "I knew you had it in you."

"I haven't decided anything yet, and I won't until I talk to Tony. This is something he needs to decide, not me, and not you, no matter how much we might want to."

"But if he agrees, you're going to kill those people."

This was it. Sam could deny it and tell Julian he would never do something like that, but that wasn't the truth anymore. He didn't know if that made him a monster or if it just made him human, but he didn't care.

For Tony, he would do this and so much more.

Tony tensed when the doors to the stairs swung open, but he relaxed when Julian and Sam came in. For some reason, Julian was bouncing on the balls of his feet and looked incredibly excited, and that made Tony wary.

He loved Julian, but sometimes, the man had strange ideas, and Tony wanted nothing to do with them. They always meant trouble, which was something Tony didn't need right now.

Instead of trying to understand what was going on with Julian, Tony turned his attention to Sam. He was looking at Tony, and Tony smiled. Sam smiled back, but he stayed away, which made Tony feel both relieved and angry.

He wanted this to stop. He wanted to be able to spend time with his mate, and for Sam to come to him without hesitating or wondering if he was going to freak out. He wanted to be able to be himself, relax, and be happy, but he couldn't. The torture had ruined him, and no matter how hard he worked to get over it, it was going to take more time.

But something was off with Sam, too. Now that Tony was looking at him, he could see that Sam was twitchy, which wasn't like him. Even though Sam and Julian loved each other, Sam didn't usually feel comfortable with his brother. They were too different, and he still couldn't accept that his brother was a professional assassin.

Or maybe he could. He was relaxed enough when he spent time in the warehouse, which Tony hoped meant he'd started to accept it. Sam had told him that he understood the need to kill people who couldn't be dealt with in any other way and that while he'd never want to do the same job, he was more than happy to let Julian and the council assassins do it. He seemed sincere, and if Tony accepted that, it meant that something else was going on.

Had Julian said or done something to make his brother uncomfortable? That wouldn't be surprising, either. It would be exactly like Julian to do something like that.

Tony found himself on his feet before he could think about it. He moved toward Sam, trying to understand what was wrong with his mate. He wanted to help, even though he wasn't sure there was anything he could do. He was certainly going to try. It was the least he could do for Sam, who had been there for him since the beginning.

He stopped once he was standing in front of Sam, who was staring at him with wide eyes. It hurt Tony that his mate was so surprised to see him come close, even though he understood why Sam felt that way. Of course he was surprised. This was the first time Tony was this close to him while they were both in their human form.

"Are you okay?" he asked.

Sam frowned. "Why wouldn't I be?"

"You don't *look* okay. There something up with you, and while you don't have to tell me if you don't want to, I'm here if you want to talk."

Sam's expression softened. "Thank you."

Tony took a step back. He needed space now that Sam knew he would do anything he could to help. He hadn't been lying, either. He wanted to be strong for Sam, and he didn't want his mate to treat him like he was fragile, even though he was in some ways. "Do you want to sit with me?" he asked.

It was hard to resist the instinct to run back to his bedroom, but he did. As long as Sam didn't try to touch him like Armand had earlier, he believed things would be okay. He wanted him and Sam to take a step forward in their relationship, even though he had no idea what that would mean, and it wouldn't happen if he couldn't stand to spend time with his mate while they both were in their human form. Gentry had warned him not to push himself too much, but that wasn't what he was doing.

Sam looked surprised, but he nodded. "I'd like nothing more."

From his expression, Tony believed him.

He and Sam settled on the couch. Tony's skin felt itchy with the closeness. It was hard to resist the urge to leave, so maybe he *was* pushing himself. He should probably slow down and try to relax, but he couldn't. He'd already given the people who had tortured him too much time, too much space in his life. He wanted it to be over. He wanted a normal life, and once again, his thoughts went to killing the people who had hurt him.

Would getting rid of them change anything? Would it help him deal with what was going on and feel more comfortable with his mate and everyone else? Tony didn't have answers to those questions, and while he wanted them, he also wanted to spend time with Sam without obsessing over what had been done to him.

Sam kept his distance, and while he chatted with the other people in the living room, it was obvious most of his attention was on Tony. It made Tony's skin prickle, although with what, he didn't know. He wanted Sam to touch him, and his werewolf would be more than okay with it. He was sure he would freak out if it happened, though, and he didn't want to do that in front of everyone else. What would Sam think if Tony asked him to go up to his bedroom? Would he assume Tony was over everything and that he wanted more?

No. That wasn't the kind of person Sam was. Ever since they'd met, Sam had made sure that Tony knew they were doing this at his pace, which meant that if Tony told him he was uncomfortable about anything, Sam would back down. He already had. Every time they were together, Sam had shifted and stuck to his rabbit form so Tony could be okay, even though it meant they couldn't talk.

Maybe it was time to change that, but they couldn't have a private conversation in the living room, which meant they had to move. Tony cleared his throat and leaned closer to Sam without touching him. "Do you think we could go to my bedroom to talk?" he asked.

Sam blinked, obviously surprised, but he nodded. "Of course."

Tony loved that Sam didn't even ask why he wanted to talk or about what. Tony had asked, and he'd said yes. It made Tony feel kind of guilty, because Sam was giving a lot to this relationship while he wasn't. He hoped that eventually, that would change. It wasn't fair to Sam that he was the only one making compromises, but for now, this was what they had to deal with.

Thankfully, no one said anything when both Sam and Tony got to their feet and headed toward the stairs. Tony turned around once, and Miles winked at him, but he didn't ask what was going on or what Tony and Sam were doing. Tony suspected everyone in the room was aware of their exit, but he focused on Sam instead of on that.

When they reached his bedroom, he left the door open when he stepped in. Sam hovered there, looking from the hallway to the bedroom. Tony had to swallow twice before he could say, "Come in, but please, leave the door open."

Sam did exactly that, walking into the bedroom and coming to a stop in the middle of it.

He was far enough away that he couldn't touch Tony without moving closer, and Tony didn't miss the fact that Sam had positioned himself so Tony could leave the room if he wanted to, and without having to come anywhere close to him.

It made Tony's chest squeeze painfully. Sam truly was ready to do just about anything for him, and Tony wanted to do anything for Sam. Instead of listening to his fear, for once, he listened to his heart. He stepped closer until he came to stand just in front of Sam. He reached for Sam, and Sam stayed still.

He was clearly afraid to do something that would send Tony running, and while Tony hated that, he was also grateful, because it meant he could lean over and gently kiss Sam on the lips. His werewolf cheered in the back of his mind, and Tony found himself smiling. "Thank you," he murmured.

Sam still wasn't moving. "What are you thanking me for?"

"For giving me time. I want to do so much more than just kiss you, but I'm not ready for anything else. I'm not even sure I'm ready for you to kiss me back."

Sam nodded. "That's why I didn't."

"But you would have if you could have?"

"Tony, I always want to kiss you. I always want to touch you and hold you close, but I know better. I don't care if it takes us years to get there. As long as you're happy, I'm happy, too."

"But you didn't look happy when you came into the living room. Did Julian do something to you?"

Sam shook his head. He looked more hesitant now, and Tony hoped it meant he was about to tell him what was going on. "It's actually something Julian said."

"Do you want to talk about it?"

"Not really, but I think we should." Sam sucked in a breath. "Do you think you'd feel better if we killed the people who tortured you?"

From Tony's expression, he hadn't expected that question. It made Sam want to take it back, but of course, he couldn't. Instead, he stared at his mate, waiting for Tony to answer.

"Why are you asking that?" Tony asked.

He sounded cautious but not angry, which gave Sam hope he wouldn't kick him out of the room.

"That's what Julian said. He was wondering if killing the people who hurt you would make it easier for you to deal with the aftermath. I know it's not a miracle solution or anything like that, and I warned him that you had to be the one making that decision, but I thought it might be worth mentioning."

"That's why he was so happy when the two of you arrived?"

"He seems to think this is the perfect solution. Sometimes, he gets a bit too excited."

"I was actually thinking about that, too."

Tony's confession surprised Sam, although maybe it shouldn't have. He knew how bad Tony felt that he had to keep Sam at a distance and that he needed to isolate himself so he wouldn't freak out. Tony wanted to go back to his old life, and while killing the people who had hurt him wouldn't miraculously heal him, it might help.

"What would you think about me if the answer was yes?" Tony continued.

"That you deserve to have a choice in this, and a life without looking over your shoulder every single step you take and without fear."

Tony frowned. "But you don't like professional assassins. You told me that."

"And if you remember, I also told you that it was because I felt I had to follow in my father's footsteps. It's basically the family business. I don't think I ever would be able to make it a job, though."

"But you still don't think badly of me for doing it?"

Sam wished he could drag Tony into his arms or maybe hold his hands. Instead, he kept his distance. "I don't think badly of you for doing it, or of Julian and my parents. I just always felt like I had to do this, even though I didn't want to. Going my own way made me feel like I wasn't part of the family, which is why I always bitched about it. I know I have to get used to it, though. You're my mate, and you're a professional assassin."

"You could just leave me behind. It would probably be easier for you."

"I'm not interested in easier. I'm interested in having you in my life, and if killing those people makes it happen, then I'm all for it."

"I'll be part of your life even if we don't do it."

"But you want to do it anyway."

Tony sighed and took a step back. He raked a hand through his hair and started pacing the room. Sam made sure they didn't touch each other every time Tony passed in front of him. He could be careful *for* Tony if Tony wasn't.

"On the one hand, I'm hoping that killing them will mean I'm not afraid anymore. If they're not there to hurt me, I can be free. On the other hand, though, I know it's not that easy. I'm terrified they'll come back for me, but I'm also scared of random people touching me and a lot of other things. Killing them won't solve that. I still have to work hard on myself, and nothing will get me out of doing that."

"But it could help. Besides, even if it doesn't, we would rid the world of someone who doesn't deserve to be in it. We could save other people from being tortured."

Tony stopped in front of Sam. He was smiling, something Sam didn't understand until Tony explained, "You truly don't have anything against this job, do you?"

"I told you I don't. I even understand the need for it. I just never wanted to do it."

"So who would kill those people? Because I don't think I can go there on my own. I hate admitting it, but I think I'll break down if I have to face them again on my own."

"I'd come with you. If you decide to do it, I'll help you."

"But you never wanted to be an assassin. You never wanted to kill people, even when it's the right thing to do, or rather, the only thing to do. I can't ask you to do this."

Sam knew he would have to think about this some more. Julian had only just suggested it, and even though Tony had accepted, it would take some time to make it happen. There was one thing Sam was sure of, though. "Whatever you need, I want to give it to you. If it means going with you to kill those people, I'll do it."

"I don't want you to do anything you don't want to or for you to hate me for pushing you into this."

"I could never hate you. I want to do this for you, but also for me."

Tony frowned. "That doesn't make sense."

Sam wasn't sure how to explain. "I always knew I didn't want to do this job, and like I said, it made me feel different. Once my brother and my sister told our parents this was what they wanted to do, Mom and Dad focused on them. They helped train Julian and Kara, but they didn't do the same for me. I resented that, and sometimes, I wonder if maybe I should just have gone along with it. Would it have been that bad?"

"You're a real estate agent."

"And I wish I wasn't. I don't like that job."

Tony's expression softened. "What job would you want to do if you could choose?"

"Not real estate agent, and not professional assassin. I think I'd like to do something to take care of people. I can't see myself finding a new job, though. This is what I studied to do." Sam was stuck with his job.

"You could study something else. You don't even have to study. You could just find another job."

"And who would hire me? What kind of job could I do? I want to take care of people, but I've never done that as a job. I'm great at organizing things, setting up open houses, dealing with people, but taking care of them? Besides, what kind of job could I find taking care of people?"

"I don't know. But why would you want to go with me to kill the men who hurt me when you want to take care of people? I don't want you to do something you hate. I don't want you to have to deal with that kind of feeling."

"Look, Tony. I'm not going to try to stop you from doing this if you feel you have to. It's your decision to make, just like choosing whether or not I want to go with you is my decision. You have to trust that I know what I'm doing." Even though Sam really didn't. He would be at a loss if he had to kill someone, but that didn't mean he couldn't stand next to Tony and support him while he did so. Maybe this was what Tony needed to do to get better. Maybe once he killed the person who had tortured him himself, it would be easier for him to move forward.

"As long as you never resent me for it." Tony still sounded skeptical.

"I know I won't, not even in the future."

"All right. I don't know if I'll be able to do it, but I'm going to try. We can't go alone, though. You don't have any experience, and while I want you to be there with me to support me, you won't be able to help if something goes wrong. I'm also not at my best, which means that if we go alone, we'll fuck it up."

"What do you suggest?"

"I think Miles should come with us."

Sam wasn't surprised. He wasn't jealous of Miles exactly. He didn't see him as a rival for Tony's affection or anything like that, but he *was* jealous of the fact that Miles had a closer relationship with Tony than Sam did at the moment. Even though Tony kept Miles at arm's length, too, he was obviously more comfortable with him than he was with anyone else.

Okay, so maybe Sam *was* jealous.

It would change. Sam was convinced of that, and he wasn't going to make an ass of himself by being jealous and rejecting Tony's idea. Besides, it was a smart one. Tony was right when he said that Sam had no experience when it came to this and that he wasn't up to dealing with problems if they arose.

"All right. Miles can come with us," Sam agreed. "Do you think he'll try to stop us?"

Tony snorted. "If I know him, he's going to be the first in line to do this for me. Killing people isn't something we do for personal gain usually, but in this case, I doubt anyone will have a problem with it."

Sam hoped they wouldn't. He wasn't sure whether this would help Tony, but if there was even a little chance it did, he wanted Tony to be able to do it. They would deal with the consequences later, once it was done. For now, they had to start planning, and while Sam wasn't looking forward to doing this, he was looking forward to Tony finally getting what he deserved and being able to leave the past behind.

CHAPTER SIX

Tony was freaking out. He'd expected something to happen, which was why he'd insisted Miles come with him and Sam. He hoped things would go smoothly, but by now, he knew better.

It had been easy to find the people who had hurt him. They all worked for the government, which made the situation even more horrifying. Win had agreed to allow Tony, Miles, and even Sam to find the man in charge and kill him, but he'd demanded he and the other assassins be allowed to deal with the others. He'd wanted to look into the fact that they'd had to obey orders, which was possibly the only reason they'd captured and helped torture him.

Tony didn't care. It didn't matter why they'd done it. Any good person would have refused to obey those orders, no matter the cost. Torturing someone was horrifying, and that was coming from a professional assassin.

Tony had never tortured anyone. He might kill people who deserved it, but he didn't take any enjoyment from it. He did his job, and that was that. If the council had ordered him to kill someone who didn't deserve it, he would have refused, no matter the personal cost.

The man he was about to kill deserved to be tortured, but Tony wouldn't lower himself that way.

Beck had been able to give Tony a home address, and everyone had agreed it would be easier and better if they killed the man at his house. There wouldn't be any guards around, but there was a security system. With Miles's help, getting around it would be easy enough.

They were doing this. *Tony* was doing this. He was going to kill the man who had given the orders to torture him, the man who had even tortured him himself. In Tony's mind, he was an unbeatable monster, but not for long. Tony had no way to know what would happen to him or how he would feel once that man was dead, but he would find out soon enough.

He was relieved he wasn't going on his own. He was pretty sure that if he had, he would have failed, and he would have gotten himself killed. That still worried him, but what worried him even more was putting Sam in danger.

This wasn't Sam's job. He wasn't trained for it, even though since they'd decided to do this, he'd spent a lot of time in the gym with his brother. It didn't make up for years of experience, and Tony was terrified he was going to get his mate hurt, or worse. He should have said no when Sam had told him he was coming along, but he wasn't sure he could do this without his mate by his side.

He and Sam were still figuring things out. Tony didn't know if he could call what they had a relationship, but they were working toward that, and he wanted it so much it made him want to throw caution to the wind and say fuck it. Even if killing the man who had tortured him didn't fix Tony's life, it would help, which was all that mattered.

A knock on his bedroom door made him jump. He forced himself to stride toward the door and opened it. This was one more step forward he had to take — not being afraid when he was in his own home. None of the people who lived here or visited would hurt him, and he had to keep that in mind.

Miles stood in front of him, smiling. "Ready?" he asked.

Tony chuckled. "I don't think I'll ever be ready, but sure. Let's go."

"Sam is downstairs waiting for us."

Tony hesitated. "Do you think it's a stupid idea?"

"What?"

"To allow Sam to come with us. He's not like us. It's not only that he's not trained, but also that he never wanted to do something like this. Am I forcing him to do it?"

Miles grabbed Tony's arm, and for once, Tony didn't want to push him away and run back to his bedroom. He needed the reassurance that he wasn't doing something inexcusable that he wouldn't be able to forgive himself for.

"You have to allow him to do what he wants," Miles said. "He's an adult, and he knows what we're about to do. If he didn't want to come, he wouldn't."

"He wants to be there for me. He wants to support me, and he thinks this is the only way to do that."

"Again, give him the benefit of the doubt. He might never have done this job, but he's been in this kind of life since he was born. He's aware of what's about to happen, yet he wants to come anyway. It's not just a guy you picked up on the streets. He's your mate, and he knows this business. He wants to be there for you, which is good."

"I never said it wasn't. I'm just worried he'll be angry and resent me for this."

"He's not going to be the one to kill that guy. If you can't do it, I will. Sam won't even have to be in the same room."

But he would insist on being there if Tony was there. Tony knew at least that about him. Miles was right, though. Sam had made his decision fully aware of what was going to happen. If he hadn't changed his mind, Tony should stop obsessing over it. The only thing he had to worry about was to keep his mate safe.

Tony and Miles headed downstairs, and just like Miles had said, Sam was waiting for them. He turned around and smiled when he heard them, but he kept his distance. He wasn't alone. Win was there, too, and so was everyone else.

They weren't coming with Tony, but he was still touched that they wanted to be there for him and show him they cared. He still couldn't get too close, so he pressed his back to the wall, grinning when Sam decided to join him.

They were so close that their hands brushed against each other. Tony kept his attention on Win, because this was it. In a few minutes, he would be out on a mission again, and even though he was nervous and expected something to go wrong, he was also excited.

"All right," Win said when he saw that everyone was looking at him. "You all know why you're here. Tony, Miles, and Sam are heading out to kill the person who gave the order for Tony to be tortured."

"I still think I should go with them," Julian grumbled.

"I agree," Win said, surprising Tony. "But Tony is the one in charge here. If he wants to go only with Miles and Sam, then that's what he's going to do." Win looked at Tony. "We're all here, and we're ready to help at any moment. Just let us know, and we'll be right with you."

Tony nodded. "I know, and I'm thankful. I need to do this on my own, or at least as much on my own as I can. I have to face that man and be the one to kill him. If I can't, Miles will do it for me. We'll keep him safe, though."

"You better," Julian snapped. He rubbed his face. Tony knew that he hadn't meant to be so harsh. He was just worried for his brother. "Sam shouldn't be doing this," he continued. "He never wanted to do it, and I don't like that he's going with you."

"I don't like this any more than you," Sam intervened. "But I'm going to do it anyway. I appreciate that you're worried about me, but it's my decision." He paused and glared at his brother. "And if you even think about telling Mom and Dad, I'll kick your ass."

That made Tony laugh, but he was still nervous, and he

knew that the sooner he killed the man who had tortured him, the better it would be. He'd be able to come back home and finally relax, which was the only thing he wanted. "We should head out," he said softly.

The room was silent as he, Miles, and Sam headed toward the door. A few people reached for Tony but stopped before they could touch him. He was thankful, even though he knew it hadn't been easy. They wanted to protect him and be there for him, but he was pushing them away.

Hopefully, that would be over soon. Killing that man wouldn't heal him from one day to another, but it would be one more step toward being free of his nightmares and going back to normal, and that was all Tony wanted.

Sam had never killed anyone, and he hadn't been planning on ever doing it — until now. Tony deserved to be the one to kill the man who had tortured him, but if he couldn't, Sam would be more than happy to step in and do it for him. He hadn't realized he was so bloodthirsty, but maybe it was a family trait. Maybe he was more similar to his parents and his siblings than he'd thought.

He wasn't sure he liked it.

The one thing he was grateful for was that his parents and his siblings had partially trained him. In the beginning, it had been something to do with Julian and Kara. They'd been kids, and it had been fun. Julian and Kara had always taken it more seriously, but Sam still remembered things, and he'd made sure to keep training over the years. He couldn't say it was because he'd been planning this, but he was glad he had. It would come in handy now, and Tony and Miles would be able to focus on what they were doing rather than on protecting him. He'd also made sure to talk to Julian before leaving, and while his brother hadn't been happy, he'd given him tips that hopefully would keep him alive and in one piece.

"Let's go over what we know one last time," Miles said.

They were headed toward the shimmering room, along with Dasha. Sam had met him recently, and he knew Dasha was the Nix that shimmered the council assassins back and forth between their home and the places they had to go to for the missions. Sam was used to shimmering, thankfully, although the rest of the situation was new.

"His name is Robert Langley," Tony murmured.

Sam moved closer to him, so close that their hands brushed together as they moved. He wasn't sure it was the right thing to do, but Tony didn't move away, so he decided to stay where he was.

"He works for the human government," Miles continued. "What did Win say? He's a colonel, or a general, or something like that."

"He's an asshole," Sam spat out.

"I think we can agree to that. Let's just call him Robert if we need to mention him."

"I thought we'd call him asshole."

Miles chuckled. "Unfortunately, there are too many people I like to call asshole, so we better stick to Robert or Langley. He should be at home right now. He lives alone, and the house is big. He has a good security system, but it shouldn't be a problem for me."

Sam should have asked what kind of power Miles had and whether he was a shifter. Almost every council assassin was, but Sam knew that the Glass Research company had also experimented on humans, so it was possible Miles wasn't. In any case, he'd come out of that lab changed, so he had at least one power, and Sam was excited to find out what it was.

"I want you two to be careful," Tony said when they reached the shimmering room. "If you feel it's too dangerous, you have to go."

Sam crossed his arms over his chest. "Are you telling us to leave you and run?"

Tony grimaced. "That's not exactly what I was saying, but yes. If you need to, leave me there and go."

"There's no way we're going to do that."

Tony's hands tightened into fists.

Sam wasn't afraid—he doubted Tony would try to hurt him. He was worried, which made sense. Sam was worried, too, but there was no way he was abandoning his mate. Whatever happened, they would make it out of that house together—all three of them.

"I'm with Sam on that," Miles said. "We're not leaving you behind, whatever happens. Besides, he's only one guy, and there's no way he knows we're coming."

"He could find out. He could shoot one of us. You don't know what's going to happen, and I wouldn't be able to live with myself if one of you got hurt because of me," Tony protested.

"It's our job."

"It might be yours, but it's not Sam's."

"But I agreed to come," Sam intervened. He didn't want Miles and Tony to fight, not over this. "I know the risks, but I still want to go with you. Let me do this for you, Tony. Let *us* do it for you."

Tony's shoulders slumped. "I know that nothing I can say will make you change your mind. That's why I haven't tried. It doesn't change the fact that I'm worried about you."

"And *we're* worried about *you*."

"We don't even know if doing this is going to change anything for me."

"Maybe not, but there's a chance it will help, even if only a bit."

Dasha cleared his throat, making all three of them jump. Sam had almost forgotten he was there, although he didn't know how he could have. Dasha was the person who would take them to Langley's house and who would pick them up once they were done. Without him, they would be in trouble.

"Are you ready?" he asked.

Sam looked at Tony, who nodded curtly. When Dasha offered his hands, all three of them touched him. Tony was obviously hesitant, but Dasha smiled sweetly at him, and Sam saw how much Tony relaxed. Tony knew Dasha. They were part of the same family, and Dasha wouldn't hurt him, whatever happened. Sam wished Tony would think the same of him, and he hoped that it would happen in time.

He would think about that once they were done, though. Right now, he had to focus on what was about to happen. He didn't want to get hurt, or for Miles and Tony to be. That meant he had to keep his head in the game, not on his future with Tony.

When they shimmered, it took him a moment to see where they'd landed. It was dark, since they were doing this during the night, and he couldn't see much, but he did see the house.

It was dark, with light coming from only a few windows. It was also isolated, which hopefully would help them, but it also made Sam worry.

Robert Langley had to have a good reason to want his house to be so out of the way. Even with all the security systems in the world, it made him vulnerable. What if someone attacked him? He wouldn't be able to get help anytime soon, which could mean death for him. Sam supposed the man wouldn't have to worry about that after tonight. Whatever his reasoning for having a house in the middle of nowhere was, Sam didn't care about it. He only cared that it gave him and the others what they needed, which was privacy and enough time to take care of Langley.

"I can stay if you want me to," Dasha murmured.

"We have this," Tony told him. "You should go back home

and wait for us to call."

"I could stick around here. I don't have to go with you in-side."

"Go home," Tony repeated. When he realized his words were maybe too harsh, he reached out and quickly squeezed Dasha's shoulder. "I know you want to help me, and I'm grateful. But if you guys had your way, you'd all be here, and this isn't a job for twenty people. As it is, we're already a crowd."

Dasha smiled and nodded. "All right. I'll go back to the warehouse and wait there. You better actually call me, though. If you don't, I'm coming to get you, and I won't be alone."

"That's what worries me," Tony said. He didn't sound worried, though. He was affectionate.

Sam could understand. All of Tony's friends had wanted to come with them to kick Langley's ass. Tony had already decided the only ones who would be with him were Sam and Miles, and he'd had to say no to everyone else. That they'd wanted to come reinforced the idea that Sam had of them as a family rather than people who shared a job. It was good to see, and hopefully, that would help Tony heal, too.

Dasha shimmered away without another word, leaving Tony, Miles, and Sam on their own. Sam had no idea what to do, so he let Tony and Miles take the lead.

He followed them toward the house, making sure to walk in their footsteps. Apparently, they knew where the cameras and motion sensors were, and even though avoiding them was complicated, it only took about ten minutes to be at the front door. Sam was stunned but relieved. The first hurdle was behind them—now came all the others.

"How are we going in?" he asked. He stared at the door, which was no doubt locked.

"Give me a moment to disable the security system," Miles

answered.

Sam looked around, but he couldn't see how Miles was going to do that. "You can do it from outside?"

Miles grinned. "You'll see."

Sam swallowed. He knew Miles wouldn't hurt him, but his answer was odd. What was he hiding?

Tony couldn't help but smile. He knew why Miles was grinning and how much he loved doing this. Usually, he didn't have an audience, so it was a treat for him. Sam, on the other hand, looked worried, so Tony leaned closer to him. "Don't worry. He knows what he's doing," he murmured.

Sam glanced over at him. "That's what worries me."

Tony chuckled softly. He was still nervous when he was close to Sam, but he was forcing himself to ignore the feeling. If he only did what he felt ready for, he and Sam wouldn't be talking. They wouldn't be together right now, and they wouldn't be getting to know each other more and more every day. It was petrifying, but the only way for Tony to trust Sam was to spend time with him, which was why he was focusing on that. Hopefully, what they were about to do would also help, although Tony wasn't too hopeful about that. He agreed that Robert Langley needed to die, but he didn't know if it would be useful to him, but even if it wasn't, he wasn't going back. He needed to do this, and he *would* do it.

They both turned toward Miles, who was waiting for them to be done talking. His smile widened and he raised a hand, wiggling his fingers so Sam would focus on them. Then, he stretched them to about twice their normal length. It was creepy as fuck.

Sam sucked in a breath. Tony knew how he felt. He could still remember the first time Miles had done this in front of him, and he'd been just as shocked. It was strange to watch

Miles stretch his limbs, no matter how many times Tony saw it.

Miles turned his attention to the door.

"That's incredible," Sam murmured.

"It is. Miles loves that this is what he ended up with once he left the labs."

"I suppose he's making the most of what was done to him."

"He is. We all try to do it."

It took Miles just a moment to get his hands under the door and wiggle them inside. He was so used to doing this by now that the door was unlocked only a few seconds later. It swung open, but Tony stayed where he was. It wasn't over yet. Before entering, they had to make sure the alarm wouldn't give up their presence.

Miles knew what he was doing. He'd specialized in breaking and entering over the years, and he was good at it. As Tony and Sam watched, he stretched his arms around the door, searching for the box that controlled the security system. He made a triumphant noise, then huffed. "I know the security system."

"Can you disable it?" Sam asked.

"I would be offended you asked, except you've never been on a mission with me. I can disable pretty much any alarm. Watch me."

When he shifted, Tony knew what to expect, and he quickly gathered the clothes that dropped on the floor. He piled them into his arms as he helped Miles wiggle out of them. Sam sucked in a breath when he saw what Miles had shifted into, and when Tony looked at him, his eyes were wide.

"What is he?" Sam asked.

"You don't recognize it?"

"It's dark, and I don't want to offend him by saying the wrong thing."

"He's an octopus."

"And what is he going to do now? Wouldn't it have been easier to disable the security system in his human form?"

"Not for him. Trust him. He's done this hundreds of times."

Miles made his way inside the house and disappeared behind the door. Tony had seen this more than once, so he knew what was happening. Miles was using his octopus body to get to the security system box on the wall. Once he was there, it would be fairly easy for him to disable everything without the motion sensors noticing him. His octopus form was much smaller than his human one

Tony waited for the beep that told him the coast was clear. As soon as he heard it, he stepped inside, dropping Miles's clothes behind the door. "You can dress," he whispered.

Sam still looked shellshocked, so Tony took his hand and pulled him inside. "You don't have to do this if you don't feel like you can." It was a lot to wrap his mind around.

Sam shook himself. "I'm not leaving."

Tony had already known he wouldn't, but he'd had to try. He was terrified something would happen to Sam or Miles, but he respected their decision, and they were in this with him.

"Ready?" Miles asked. He stepped from behind the door dressed and looking like he was ready to kick ass.

He probably was. Win had warned them to go in and out and focus on killing Robert Langley, and Miles had been disappointed he wouldn't be able to torture him the way he had tortured Tony. Tony wasn't sure what he wanted except for Robert Langley to be dead. He didn't think he could torture anyone, so he was relieved they wouldn't have time to even think about it. The sooner he was out of this house, the better he would feel.

They crept around the house, Sam behind Miles and Tony.

Tony was relieved he wasn't trying to be more active and that he was more than happy to follow the orders Tony and Miles were giving him. He might not know what he was doing, but he wasn't an idiot.

They passed a wide living room and a kitchen that was so clean it looked like no one had used it in a while. The house was empty of personal touches like pictures or books, and it made Tony's stomach churn. He trusted Beck's abilities to find out where Robert Langley lived, but it wouldn't be the first time someone realized what was happening and disappeared too soon.

"I see a light down the hallway," Miles murmured.

Tony focused on that. All the doors in the hallway were closed, but sure enough, a light came from under one of them. "What room is that?"

"The office," Sam answered.

The three of them had been briefed by Win and Beck, so they knew the layout of the house. Tony wasn't surprised that Sam remembered it well. It was his job, after all.

"Let's go," Miles said as he bounced on the balls of his feet.

When they reached the door, Miles and Sam both stepped to the side. Tony knew he was meant to do this, but his hands trembled as he reached forward. Now that he was here and about to face the man who had tortured him and had taken glee in it, he didn't know if he could do it.

A warm hand landed on the small of his back. Tony twisted to the side to see that it was Sam who was frowning. "You're still sure you want to do this?" he asked, his voice even softer than before.

Tony wasn't, but he nodded. "I have to do it."

"You don't have to do anything. I'm sure Miles will be more than happy to do it for you."

He was right, but Tony felt like this was the next step in his healing. If he avoided it, it would make everything harder, and he didn't want that to happen. He had a chance at happiness with his mate and his family. He wasn't going to give it up, even though he was terrified.

He raised his hand and reached for the handle. He wrapped his fingers around it, ignoring the way they were still trembling, and twisted to open the door.

It creaked a bit. It would have worried Tony if he and the others hadn't been about to kill the only person present in the house.

That person was behind the desk, but he shot to his feet as soon as he heard the door. He reached for his desk, and Tony acted on instinct, just like he had once done when he was on missions. It only took one thought to freeze Robert Langley from the head down. He couldn't move, except for his face, and he stared as Tony, Sam, and Miles walked in.

Sam had no idea what was next, but he followed Tony and Miles inside. He tried to appear as if he knew what was going on, but in truth, he was terrified. Luckily for him, he didn't actually have to do anything right now. He just had to be there for Tony, which was the easiest thing in the world for him to do.

He was also impressed. Tony had told him what he could do, but seeing it at work had left him awed. Tony had acted on instinct, and there had been no hint of fear in his movements or expression. He was nothing like the Tony Sam was used to, and it was kind of hot.

"Who are you?" the asshole behind the desk asked. Sam wasn't about to call him Robert, not even in his mind.

Langley was still trying to reach for his desk, no doubt to grab a weapon or his phone, but he was entirely frozen. His lips were already turning blue, and Sam couldn't think of anything more entertaining than watching him freeze to death.

He was pretty sure that wasn't how Tony was going to do things, though.

Tony stepped forward. Sam had been watching him for weeks now, so he noticed the signs that he was nervous, but he doubted Langley did.

"Remember me?" Tony asked.

Langley's eyes narrowed for a moment before they widened. "Of course. You're the reason we finally managed to get to the council assassins."

"You didn't do a great job. All of us are still alive, and we're healed. We have a new place, too, and it's even better than the first one."

"Are *you* healed, too? I did a fine job on you."

Sam stepped forward before he could even think about it. He only knew he wanted to hurt Langley and to make him feel what Tony had felt. Tony raised a hand to stop Sam, though, and Sam froze. Tony never looked at him, but Sam was pretty sure he wasn't angry at him, just trying to stop him from doing something he would regret.

"I'm perfectly fine, as you can see," Tony answered.

"Pity. I should have worked harder, but I suppose it wasn't my fault, since you managed to escape."

"Why did you try to destroy the council assassins?" Miles asked.

"Because you've been ruining everything. You killed people I needed, and I couldn't allow that to continue."

"Ruining everything? We only kill the people the council needs dead. That always means people who are a danger to shifters and the paranormal world in general."

Langley snorted. "A danger? You and your people are a danger to humanity. We shouldn't have allowed you to be part of society, and I'm going to make sure it ends."

Sam's stomach churned, and he was pretty sure he might be about to throw up. "You want to kill all shifters?" he asked.

That was what it sounded like to Sam.

Langley grinned. "If I have my way, yes. The world wasn't made for shifters. It was made for humans, and we need to get rid of you."

"We're human beings, too." How could Langley talk about killing thousands of people that way? He sounded like he truly didn't care, and Sam couldn't begin to wrap his mind around that.

"You wouldn't be able to become animals if you were human beings."

Sam took a step back. He'd expected something nasty to happen, but not this.

He wasn't new to this kind of discrimination. Some people refused to work with him because he was a shifter, and they made sure he knew that was the reason. No one had ever spewed so much hate in his face before, though, and he didn't know how to react.

"Well, you won't hurt anyone else ever again," Tony said. His voice was hard now.

Sam suspected that this was it. They were about to kill Langley, and even though he'd been hesitant before, he would be more than happy to help right now. The man was a monster, and not only because of what he'd done to Tony. He saw shifters as nothing more than animals, and he wouldn't hesitate to kill them if he could.

Instead, a shifter was going to kill him. The irony was sweet, and even though Sam knew himself well enough to be aware of the fact that he would never be comfortable with this job and that he would never do it himself, he was happy to be here right now. He wanted to see Langley die and to make sure the man would never be able to hurt anyone again.

"Even if you kill me, this isn't going to stop. Do you really think the government is okay with shifters being around? We've been working for years to make sure you don't have any more power than you already have, and we're almost done. We're going to get rid of you, and there's nothing you'll be able to do to stop us."

Tony moved forward. Langley was starting to thaw, and drops of water dripped down his body and onto his desk. He still didn't look afraid, which made Sam wonder if he was even more of a monster than Sam had thought.

"I'm going to stop you," Tony told Langley.

"But I'm not alone. You won't be able to stop all of us before we kill you."

"Maybe not, but we're going to try."

Sam had been stunned by Tony's power, but he was even more so when Tony shifted. He'd already known Tony was a werewolf, but he didn't know any werewolves personally, and he'd never seen one in their shifted form.

It was impressive, and it would have been terrifying if he hadn't known it was Tony, but Tony wouldn't do anything to hurt him and Miles.

He was right. Tony didn't even look at them. Instead, he focused on Langley, who seemed to finally realize that he wouldn't make it out of this. No matter how hard he tried to move back, he was stuck. Tony prowled toward him, flashing his fangs. If he was about to tear Langley into pieces, Sam would make sure he brushed his teeth before they kissed.

"I can give you information," Langley rushed out. "I can tell you who's involved and what we're planning."

There was panic in his voice now, and Sam smiled. Maybe he truly was bloodthirsty, and right now, he didn't care.

Tony growled, but it was Miles who answered. "We'll find out who's involved in what anyway. We don't need you."

Tony straightened to his full height and swiped his hand — paw — forward. Langley screeched, but the sound was cut off, replaced by a gurgle. Sam knew what he would see if he looked at Langley, so he made sure not to. He might have wanted Langley to die, but it didn't mean he wanted to *see* it.

"I'm going to go through his desk and computer if I can," Miles said. He moved forward, ignoring Sam and Tony.

Sam was relieved. He wasn't sure what to do or say. He'd wanted to be here when this happened, and he was happy that Tony had gotten his revenge, but Sam hadn't actually done anything.

"You should clean up," Miles continued. He was already behind the desk. "Although, can you thaw him out first? It's not going to be easy to go through his desk if I can't get to it."

Sam kept his gaze on the rest of the room. He heard a rush of water, then a thump, no doubt the body hitting the floor. He had to swallow a few times so he wouldn't throw up, and he jerked when something touched his arm.

Tony was there, looking hesitant. He was in his human form again, and while his clothes were torn, they covered everything they were supposed to cover. He'd cleaned up the blood from his hand, thankfully, and Sam turned fully toward him. "How are you feeling?" he asked.

Tony shrugged. "I'm not sure. I'm relieved he's dead and that he'll never be able to hurt me again, but what he said is a problem."

"I agree. Let's hope we can find something in his computer."

Tony reached for Sam, but he stopped before touching him. Sam thought it was because he didn't feel ready to touch anyone, so he was surprised when Tony asked, "Can I touch you?"

"Of course. You never have to ask that."

"I thought you might be afraid of me."

Sam blinked. "Because of what you just did?"

"I killed a man in front of you. I tore his throat out, and I don't regret it. I wouldn't blame you for being scared."

Since Tony wanted to touch Sam, Sam moved toward him,

taking the hand he'd used to kill Langley. Tony tried to pull back, but Sam didn't let go. "I'm not afraid of you." He raised Tony's hand to his lips and kissed the back, then the knuckles. "Nothing you can do or say will make me scared of you. I understand why you did what you did, and I approve."

Tony heavily swallowed as he nodded. "Okay. If you're sure, I guess we'll see where things go from here."

Sam knew where he wanted things to go between them, but he was pretty sure he would overwhelm Tony if he mentioned it. Instead, he limited himself to nod, too. "We'll see where things go," he agreed.

Now that Langley was dead and that Tony didn't have his presence hovering in the back of his mind anymore, it would be easier for them to get to know each other, and hopefully, to finally get together. Sam was worried about what Langley had said, but for now, he only wanted to focus on Tony.

Everything else would still be there tomorrow and the day after that. Bad things never just faded into the background.

CHAPTER SEVEN

Tony felt better.

Just like he'd expected, killing Robert Langley hadn't worked miracles. He was still afraid of leaving the house, but at least now, he could leave his bedroom. It made him nervous, but he was learning to deal with that, and even though some days he decided to stay in his room and avoided everyone, he was making progress.

It would take time, but Tony was finally moving forward instead of staying where he was or worse, moving backward. Having Sam helped, although Tony wished he could give Sam more than he could.

He was more comfortable with touch now, and they kissed as often as possible, but yesterday, Sam had tried to sneak his hand under Tony's t-shirt while they were making out, and he'd touched a scar on Tony's stomach. Tony had freaked out and pushed Sam away, and Sam had tumbled to the floor.

Sam hadn't cared. He'd been more worried about how Tony was than the fact that he'd ended up on the floor, and Tony wondered how he'd ended up with such a perfect mate. Sam truly was the right man for him. He had the patience of a saint, but he also made sure to push Tony here and there, just enough that Tony continued moving forward but not so much that he freaked out.

Tony still felt guilty about not giving Sam everything, but he knew that he would work up to it in time. Until then, kissing was good, as was learning to allow Sam to touch him. The rabbit cuddles made that even easier, and Tony smiled as he looked down at Sam, who was bundled up in his lap, sleeping.

He stroked his fingertips down Sam's back, causing him to blink his eyes open. Sam's fur was soft under Tony's skin, and it made him want more, but he knew that if Sam shifted, he would freak out. Tony wasn't ready for more than this, and thankfully, Sam understood.

"Why don't you shift?" Tony asked.

Sam cocked his head, and Tony could almost hear him asking if Tony was sure.

"I'm not entirely sure how I'll react, but I think it's time. I can deal with you in your rabbit form, and I should be able to deal with you in your human form, too. We can kiss and see what happens. I'm not ready for more, but this, I know I can do."

Sam arched a brow.

Tony huffed. "I'm sorry for throwing you to the floor yesterday, and I promise it won't happen again. As long as you keep your hands to yourself, this should be okay." He paused and frowned. "Although that's not fair. I can touch you, but you can't touch me. If you want to shift and dress right away, you can do that."

Sam had recently started shifting in Tony's private bathroom. That way, he wouldn't have to get naked in the middle of the hallway. Julian was still whining about the one time he'd seen his brother standing there naked and how he needed brain bleach, which Tony found hilarious. Still, it had pushed him to welcome Sam into his bedroom, and even though so far Sam hadn't spent the night, Tony was working toward that, too. The next step would be to have Sam naked in the same room as him, and while he was nervous, he also couldn't wait.

He liked Sam. He was pretty sure he was falling in love with Sam, although it was hard to stop obsessing over his fears and focus on that. It was too soon to say it out loud, too, especially when the words terrified Tony, but he knew how he felt, and he was pretty sure Sam felt the same way. He wouldn't be giving Tony so much leeway if he didn't.

Sam wiggled his way off Tony's lap and came to sit next to him on the bed. He looked at Tony one last time, and Tony nodded. He was never going to be readier than he already was.

Sam shifted. Instead of looking away like he usually did, Tony stared, and he was happy he had when he saw Sam's body. Sam wasn't as muscled and well-built as almost everyone who lived in the warehouse, but that was okay, because Tony loved that he wasn't. His body was thin but soft, and its sight made Tony want to touch. He reached out before he could think better about it, but he froze before touching Sam's chest. It was hairy, and Tony longed to bury his fingers there. He wouldn't do that without Sam's approval, though.

"Go ahead. I'll stay as still as I can," Sam croaked.

Tony moved. His fingertips touched Sam's chest, and Tony relaxed. Sam was warm and soft under him, and he wanted so much more. He knew better than to push too much, though. He didn't want to freak out like he had yesterday. He wanted to enjoy this moment, maybe to get a little more. "Can I kiss you?" he asked.

"Always."

Tony got onto his knees and leaned closer to Sam. He was still only touching his chest, but he had to move his hand to Sam's shoulder so he wouldn't fall against Sam. Their lips touched, and Tony sighed happily.

Once, he wouldn't have hesitated to get naked with Sam and roll around the bed with him. Now, he couldn't do that, not if he didn't want to have to lock himself in the bathroom for the next hour or so. He had to make do with what he was able to do, which was only kissing for now. It was something, though, and much more than what he'd been able to deal with only a month ago. No matter how frustrating it was, this was the right way to do it.

A knock on the door interrupted them. Tony groaned and straightened, turning to glare at it. "What?" he snapped, expecting Miles or Julian to be on the other side.

"I'm sorry if I'm interrupting something," Win said. He sounded amused, thankfully.

Tony sighed. "You're not. Can I help you with something?"

"I'd like to talk to Sam, if it's possible. I'll be waiting downstairs. You're welcome to be part of the conversation."

Tony frowned and turned to face Sam. "Do you know what he's talking about?"

"Not yet. We'll be right there," Sam added, raising his voice so Win could hear him.

Tony was nervous, and as soon as Sam was dressed, he grabbed his hand and squeezed. He didn't think anything bad was about to happen, especially since Win had sounded light-hearted, but he was still wary. It was a consequence of the torture, and he was learning to deal with that, too, but it was harder than he wished it was.

He and Sam made their way downstairs. Tony wasn't afraid to leave his bedroom anymore, although he was always careful that no one came too close to him. If there was a possibility he could freak out with his mate, he knew he *would* do so if anyone else did. Thankfully, his family was good at keeping their distance even as they made him feel like he was still one of them. He'd thought he'd lost all of this after he'd escaped, but now, he realized he hadn't and that he never would. He still hated what had been done to him, but it had shown him how strong he was, how much other people cared for him, and of course, it had given him Sam.

Win and Roark were sitting at the dining table, sipping on coffee. They both looked up and smiled when they heard Sam and Tony. It helped Tony relax because now he was sure nothing bad was about to happen.

"Why don't you sit down?" Roark said, gesturing at the empty chairs around the table.

A few people were on the couch watching TV, and Graham was cooking, but no one even turned to look at them, and that, too, helped Tony relax.

He and Sam sat next to each other, and Tony reached for Sam's hand under the table. Sam had no idea what was happening either, and he had to be nervous. He was visiting almost every day, but Tony knew that being surrounded by professional assassins still made him nervous, probably because he knew they wouldn't hesitate to hurt him if he did anything to hurt Tony.

Maybe Tony should have a conversation with everyone before the next time Sam came around.

"So, Roark and I have been talking," Win started. "As Tony already knows, and I'm sure you've noticed, Sam, both he and I are extremely busy, especially with all the information the three of you brought back from Langley's house. Usually, we split up taking care of the household, but we haven't been able to do that lately, and it's catching up on us."

Tony had no idea where he was going with that. "What do you mean?" he asked.

"We've always been the ones who took care of everything, from grocery shopping to making sure everything in the house works right, to giving everyone a listening ear if they needed it. Of course, we still want to do that, but with the work being what it is and more people moving into the warehouse as every council assassin finds their mate, it's getting to be too much. Beck has taken on some of the work when he became our computer expert, and of course, Graham took cooking out of everyone's hands, but we need more, and we'd like to offer Sam a job."

Sam blinked. "What do you mean?"

"We've been talking, and I'm sure you noticed that we've asked you pointed questions lately."

"I did think it was weird, but I was afraid to ask why you were asking them."

"We know you're a great organizer, which is definitely needed when it comes to this job. You've also integrated yourself extremely well with the others, and that gives us hope that you'll be able to deal with this. We have a list of things we usually do and are planning on unloading on to you if you're okay with it, and of course, if you accept the job. It would be paid, and you'll have a room here to live with us until you and Tony feel ready to move in together. We're ready to consider someone else if you refuse, but you're Tony's mate, and we think it would be better to keep this job in the family, so to speak."

"This is overwhelming." Sam sounded stunned.

Tony understood why. It was overwhelming for him, too. He wasn't sure whether Roark and Win really needed someone to do this job or if they were just giving Sam and Tony a chance to spend more time together, but he was grateful either way. Sam didn't like his job, and Tony knew he would quit if he had another lined up.

Now, he did.

"We understand," Roark continued. "You don't have to answer right away, of course, but we'd like you to think about it." He pushed a folder that had been on the table in front of him toward Sam. "Go over all of this. Ask as many questions as you need or want. When you're ready, give us your answer. We'd like it to be as soon as possible, since we're overrun with work and barely have time to spend with our mates and family, but take as much time as you need."

Sam slid the folder closer, but he didn't open it. "I'll go over it," he promised.

"Good."

"And I'll talk with Tony about it. He should have a say in whether or not I move in."

Tony's heart felt so full that it might be about to explode. He wasn't surprised that Sam was thinking about him and his reaction to this, but he thought it was sweet. *Sam* was sweet, and Tony couldn't wait to see what would happen next between them.

It wouldn't be easy, but then, nothing in Tony's life ever was. That didn't mean it wasn't worth it. With Sam living in the warehouse, they would have the opportunity to spend more time together, and Tony couldn't wait.

He wasn't healed by any means, but he was getting there, and he couldn't wait to see what the future would be like now that Sam was in his life.

You may also enjoy the following from eXtasy Books Inc:

Niall
Catherine Lievens

Excerpt

Niall's father was hiding something. Niall had no idea what it was, but he wanted to find out. He needed to find out because he wasn't ready to lose his father, and he was afraid he might.

He couldn't stop thinking about it. After losing his mother ten years ago to breast cancer, he was terrified of something similar happening to his father. It would be just like the man to hide health problems from his children to protect them, even though all three of them would be angry. The fact that Niall's father was hiding something pointed at that, and Niall had no idea how to find out what was happening. He knew his father, and if he pushed, his dad would clam up.

"Watch out!"

Niall just had the time to crunch forward. He felt something move above his head, and he stayed still until he was sure the danger was gone. When he straightened and turned around, he found his best friend glaring at him.

"I told you I was coming in with this," he said, gesturing at the beam of wood he was carrying on one shoulder.

Niall hadn't heard him. If he was honest, he had no idea what was happening around him, which was a problem considering his job.

He sighed and rubbed his face. "I'm sorry. I didn't hear you."

Val stared at him for so long that Niall wondered if he was going to try to hit him with that beam. Instead, he put it down, even though Niall was pretty sure that wasn't where the beam was supposed to go. Val didn't seem to care, and he came toward Niall, peering at him. "What's going on?"

Niall shook his head. "Nothing." He had nothing to say, not when he didn't know what was happening to his father.

"Bullshit. Something is going on, and I'm getting worried. Usually, you wouldn't hesitate to tell me." Val paused. "Unless it has something to do with me?"

"You're not the center of the universe."

That made Val smile. "Simon would disagree."

"That's because he's smitten with you."

"I would be worried if he weren't considering he's my mate." Niall had hoped Val was done interrogating him, but he should have known better because he continued, "You'd tell me if something was wrong with you, right?"

"You're my best friend. Of course I would." And Niall should probably talk to someone about this. The best people to do it with would be his siblings, but he was closer to Val. "Maybe we can talk after work?"

"We should, but you have to survive until then. It's not like you to be distracted."

"I promise I'll be more careful." If Niall's father really had health problems, the last thing their family needed was for Niall to get hurt.

He did his best to focus on the work once he and Val were done talking. Luckily, they were in charge of this team, so no one had anything to say about them taking a five-minute break to talk, especially after the way Niall had been behaving. Niall was pretty sure most of the team was worried about him, and he made extra effort to focus on the work and on his coworkers instead of obsessing over his father. Whatever was happening, there was nothing Niall could do right now. Worrying wasn't going to help, and his father would kick his ass if he found out that Niall had been so distracted he'd almost taken a wooden beam to the head.

Niall was relieved when work was finally over. He let Val talk to the owners of the house they were working on today and started cleaning up. He wasn't in the mood to talk to anyone, even though technically, it was his job since his uncle owned the company he and Val worked for. His uncle had always liked Val best when it came to the job, though, and Niall didn't mind.

"Okay," Val said when he got back to Niall. "What's going on?"

"Not here," Niall murmured. He didn't want the customers to overhear a personal conversation.

Val nodded. "How about we grab something for lunch? I'll tell Simon I won't be home until tonight."

"He won't care?"

Val beamed, just like always when he spoke of his mate. "He's not my jailer. He loves me, and he understands I have other people in my life, including you."

Niall was relieved Simon hadn't demanded Val stop being friends with him or something like that when they'd bonded. He'd been wary of Val finding out he was a shifter's mate, and he still was. He had no idea what to expect when it came to shifters, at least not in real life. He knew the theory, just like everyone else, but when it came to his best friend, it wasn't enough.

There was nothing he could do about it. Val knew that Niall wasn't sure how he felt about shifters, but he hadn't considered that when he'd decided to bond with Simon. Niall hadn't expected him to. Val was an adult, and he knew what he was doing better than Niall. Besides, he was happy with

Simon. The relationship between Val and Niall had changed since Simon had become part of Val's life, but then, it would have changed even if Simon hadn't been a shifter and if Val hadn't been his mate.

"Let's grab something for lunch," Niall agreed.

Val was already texting, no doubt telling Simon that something was wrong with Niall and that he was going to try to get information out of him. Niall didn't mind, although he wasn't sure how he felt about Val telling Simon what was going on with him.

Niall realized it was his fault he didn't know Simon well yet. Simon and Val hadn't been together long, but it had been several months, and he should know his best friend's mate better than he did. He needed to change that, but not right now. Now, he had to focus on his father, and Val might be able to help.

They drove to the dinner separately, each of them taking their own truck. That way, once they were done, Niall could head back to work while Val visited Simon for a quickie or whatever he was planning.

"What's going on?" Val asked once they were seated at a table, both of them holding a glass of water.

Niall took a sip, trying to put how worried he was into words that made sense. Val knew Niall's family, and he would be worried, too. Maybe there was no reason to hide the fear. "My father is hiding something," Niall said.

Val blinked. He waited for a moment, maybe for Niall to continue. When Niall didn't, he frowned. "What's going on with Regan?"

"I don't know. That's the problem. He's been acting weird, and I know he's hiding something."

"But you don't know what it is."

"That's what scares me. What if he's sick and doesn't want to tell us?"

Understanding dawned on Val's face. "You think it's cancer?"

"I don't know. I haven't tried talking to him yet, but it's obvious there's something he's not telling us. He's not answering his phone as often as usual, and he's also not calling as much. I went to visit him the other day, and he wouldn't let me in. He was flustered. He said the floors were wet, but he was only wearing sweatpants."

"Maybe he was doing something and he didn't want you to find out."

Niall grimaced, understanding what Val was implying. "Maybe." After all, his father was an adult, but Niall didn't want to think about his father in relation to anything sexual. "But mom died ten years ago. He would have been doing that even before now. No, this is a recent change."

"How recent?"

"I don't know for sure. I realized about a month ago."

"And you've been keeping that to yourself until now?"

Niall shrugged and took another sip of water. "You had other things to focus on. You just moved in with Simon, and you're still in your honeymoon period. I didn't want to bother you."

Val reached out and slapped the back of Niall's head. "You wouldn't have bothered me. This is your father we're talking about. I want to find out what's happening. I care about him, even though he's not my father."

"I know, but I don't have anything else to tell you. I have no idea what's going on."

"You should talk to him, and to Flynn and Shona. It involves them, too. Whatever your father is hiding, if it involves his health, they need to know."

He was right. Niall should have talked to them before now, but he hadn't wanted to worry them. He was going to have to, though. This was a family matter, and they needed to be involved. "I'll text them to see when they're available. We can get together and talk about this before we confront Dad."

"Exactly. Maybe they know something you don't. Maybe you're worrying for nothing."

Niall hoped Val was right, but he couldn't dismiss the niggle of worry and dread that had hooked itself in the back of his mind. He'd already lost his mother. He didn't know what he would do if he lost his father, too.

ABOUT THE AUTHOR

Catherine is the creator of several series, most of them paranormal, including the Whitedell Pride Series and the Gillham Pack Series. While she graduated in translation, she decided to go the writer's way because it was more fun to create her own stories and characters.

She's been living in Italy for more than twenty years, but she's a daughter of the North—Belgium to be precise—and she misses it so much that she's already planning to move back.

She loves pizza—probably too much—her son, her pets, and of course, books. She sneaks some reading time into her schedule every time she has five minutes free from writing, demands from her various pets and son, and lastly, housework.

Connect with her:

lievens.catherine@gmail.com
BookBub: https://www.bookbub.com/authors/catherine-lievens
Website: https://authorcatherinelievens.com/
Facebook: https://www.facebook.com/catherine.lievens.9
Facebook Group: https://www.facebook.com/groups/411788002341528/
Twitter: https://twitter.com/authorCLievens
Newsletter: http://eepurl.com/c-uvKn